THE DARK LORD BERT

CHRIS FOX

CHRIS FOX WRITES LLC

ISBN-13: 978-1-79-667905-2

For anyone who's ever slung dice
with their gaming buddies.

BERT SMART

Bert trudged up the steep ridge, swaying briefly as the wind caught his oversized pack. He wasn't very strong, and he wasn't very fast, but that was sort of expected when you were a goblin. Not a full warg rider, or a spear thrower, or even a G Biter.

No, Bert was the lowest of the low. He was just a 1-hit-point goblin, so low that adventurers couldn't even see him, since he counted as a critter, like a rabbit or one of those cute, little owls.

But Bert had one advantage. An advantage that he would use to outsmart the village elders, and even his mom. An advantage he'd cultivated from the very weakness that caused the bigger goblins to laugh at him.

He smiled wickedly, and reveled in his own power. "Bert smart."

Bert finally crested the ridge, and hurried over to a ledge so he could peer down into the small, pine-covered ravine below. Thick trunks carpeted the steep slopes below him, all the way to the valley floor where a titanic combat was about to play out.

On one side stood an adult red dragon, its scarlet scales gleaming under the early morning sunlight. On the other stood the adventuring party that Bert had been following for the last three days. All four heroes were veterans of many battles. Bert should know. He'd been following them off and on for months.

In the lead stood a mighty dwarf paladin, his thick, rust-colored beard and bushy hair combining into something resembling a lion's mane. The dwarf's plate armor clanked as he cautiously advanced toward the dragon, all the while beating his sword on his shield to get the beast's attention. A bright red oval stone shone from the trope socket set into the dwarf's chest, and Bert knew if he crept close enough he'd be able to see the sigil emblazoned on the trope. He wanted to add it to his catalogue, but hadn't yet had an opportunity to get close enough to study it.

Behind the dwarf stood an elven ranger, his long, blond locks fluttering in the wind. Long, pale ears curved up behind a narrow face, and a sickly white light shone from his trope. That one Bert had already inspected, while the elf was passed out after drinking, which was pretty much always. The trope was emblazoned with a little stick man with a sad face holding a bow.

Emblazoned. Bert liked that word.

The elf cradled his bow loosely in one hand, and used the other to deftly pluck a trio of arrows from his quiver. The very instant those arrows left the quiver three more sprang into their place, added by the quiver's magic. He nocked all three arrows and took aim at the dragon.

"Why have you come here?" the dragon roared, its deep voice echoing up the steep slopes. "I bother no one. I hunt only animals, and only in the deep forests. I present no threat to—"

The elf loosed all three arrows, each winging off in a different direction like a bird, their magic allowing them to twist and dodge around tree branches. They arced around, then came at the dragon from three separate directions.

The dragon saw the projectiles coming, and vaulted into the air with a mighty flap of its leathery wings. The beast hovered there, but the arrows simply adjusted course. All three flew unerringly toward the same place on the dragon's body, and Bert winced sympathetically as the arrows thudded into the dragon's crotch in rapid succession.

The beast gave a high-pitched screech, and its fore-claws dropped to cover the affected region. Its slitted eyes narrowed, and it fixed its baleful gaze on the elf. "You honorless cur."

"Dude, it's a curse," the elf protested with an apologetic shrug. "It isn't my fault. I have no choice. The arrows always go right for the crotch. Sorry, man."

Confident he was far enough to be outside the splash zone of any area-of-effect attacks, Bert set down his pack and removed his blanket. He rolled it carefully out on the ground, and withdrew a small leather sack with his lunch. Bert pulled the wrapping from his sandwich, and began to chew as he watched the fight play out below.

The dragon was too high for the dwarf to reach, but the two casters in the rear of the party had no such issues. The first to act was the party's leader, as Bert understood it.

They called him Master White, which made sense since he wore white robes. Theoretically, at least. The robes were badly stained with blood, soot, and dirt, all caked in layers. But here and there you could still see patches of white.

Master White raised both hands and began chanting in a strange language Bert didn't understand. "*Eplurbus Enum ad hoc carpe diem.*"

Dark, malevolent energies seeped from the necromancer into the trees around him, which began to wither and die. Those energies gathered around White in a swirling corona of power. He gathered the dark spell and flung it at the dragon.

The spell slammed into the poor creature's chest, and the magic exploded outwards, washing over every part of the creature. The beast screeched again, this time more weakly. Its rich scarlet scales faded to a pallid grey, and its wingbeats were too weak to keep it aloft. The dragon plummeted, clawing desperately at a tall pine that cracked under its weight.

The beast tumbled heavily to the valley floor, one wing giving a tremendous crack as it shattered under the dragon's body.

"Finally!" the dwarf roared, charging the stunned beast. He leapt onto its back, and rammed his sword into the dragon's eye. The beast weakly swatted the dwarf away, and he tumbled backward, but came to his feet laughing. "That's right! Yer half blind. Dropped yer AC by two, and you gain the flanked condition, even against a single opponent."

Bert knew that AC was short for 'armor class,' but he had no idea what a flanked condition was. The adventurers were always talking about rules, most of which Bert didn't understand.

The final caster, a slender elven sorceress with platinum hair and glittering sapphire eyes, stood just outside the swathe of dead trees killed by the white necromancer. She raised her staff and began to chant in the same strange language the necromancer had used. "*Lorem ipsum dolor sit amet.*"

A wave of golden energy washed out from her staff, and settled over her and her companions. The effect was immediate. All four began to vibrate, and every step they took came far more swiftly, though to Bert's mind the haste spell seemed like overkill.

The ranger loosed another volley of arrows, which unerringly slammed into the doomed dragon's crotch. It screeched again, and desperately sought to cover its nads, to no avail.

The dwarf seized the dragon's head, and rammed his sword into its remaining eye. "Ha! Yer fully blind. Now you've got a 50% miss chance and you have to guess our square."

Bert expected the necromancer to cast another hideous spell, but instead White bravely ran into the dragon's lair, a wide cave mouth just behind where the dragon was making its last stand.

Bert carefully folded the sandwich wrapper and placed it back in his sack. It would take the adventurers a while to go through the treasure, but when they were done he could have his fill of whatever they left behind.

There would be copper. So much glorious copper.

2

THE GAME

K it peered up the ridge, through the sun-dappled pines, but saw no movement. There were a few critters, but no adventurers or monsters. Nothing that could threaten their party, at least. So why did she feel compelled to keep glancing up the wooded slope?

"What is it?" Master White called. The necromancer moved to stand near her, and she gagged reflexively at the odor that emanated from his robes, which hadn't been laundered since the river they'd passed early last week. White stared up at the ridge, shading his eyes with one delicately manicured hand. "Anything worth XP? I still have plenty of spells left for the day."

"No, just a feeling," Kit admitted. She gave up and turned back to the dragon's lair, unsurprised that both Brakestuff and Crotchshot had already disappeared inside. The best loot was likely already spoken for, but then that was always the case. "I just can't shake the feeling we're being watched, but if we are they're either a high-level rogue, or maybe they're using an invisibility spell."

"Why don't you cast a see invisibility then?" Master

White demanded in a tone that made it clear she should have thought of that. He stroked at his goatee, judge-ily. Was that a word? It was now. "If they're powerful enough to cast it, then they're high enough level to give us XP."

"Uh, because you won't let me memorize it?" Kit eyed him sidelong. "See invisibility is second level. You wanted me to memorize bull's strength and politician's rhetoric, so that I could buff you and Brakestuff. Besides, aren't you a caster too? Why don't you cast it?"

"I am no common wizard or sorcerer." White seized the lapels of his necromancer's robes and displayed them proudly. They bore a stylized hand with only its middle finger raised, the mark of the OLP, the magical organization he belonged to. They were so secretive no one knew what the letters stood for. "I've been recognized as a white necromancer. My time is spent mastering the whispered arts, so that I can call upon my ancestors for aid. It is a noble calling, one only the most lawful and righteous are allowed to practice."

Kit gave a disgusted sigh, and started toward the cave. She'd had this argument too many times, and wasn't interested in another helping of White's arrogance.

She dimly sensed that this, all of this, wasn't real. They were playing some sort of game, and White was someone she knew back in the real world. But the magic of the game obscured everything that wasn't part of it, so as not to ruin the immersion.

Crotchshot and Brakestuff were also people she knew in the real world, though how or why wasn't clear, thanks to the game.

Both companions were scooping gold into Brake's backpack as fast as they could shovel it. The tan-colored haversack was magical in nature, and could hold much more than it appeared. So much so that even they struggled to fill it.

"I take it neither of you counted the money before you shoved it inside?" she asked, though Kit already knew the answer.

"Nah. Master White will deal with that when we get to camp." Brakestuff waved dismissively at her. "I'm more interested in the magic stuff. There's a shield and a ring."

"Any tropes?" Kit moved to the small pile of gear they'd accumulated, and then muttered a detect magic spell. Several objects began to glow, which included the shield and the ring.

"Nah," Crotchshot looked a little crestfallen. "That was the first thing I looked for."

"I thought you liked your trope." Kit bent to inspect the ring, a simple, gold band with a single emerald.

"I do like it, mostly. I mean, I even chose my name around the flaw. It isn't so bad," the ranger replied as he scooped the rest of the gold into the haversack. "Shooting people in the crotch isn't really a disadvantage, unless we run into something with no discernible anatomy. Then there's nothing for the curse to latch onto and my bow doesn't work. If we run into a gelatinous cube, you're on your own."

Master White's faint musk preceded the necromancer, and she turned to face the tall, dark-haired man as he entered the cave. White was handsome, and one of the most charismatic people she'd ever met. The robes were so out of keeping, but they didn't give a penalty to social checks, and all White cared about was numbers.

He stared down at the loot for a moment, then looked up at her. "What does the ring do?"

Kit turned and held it up for his inspection. "It's a lesser ring of wizardry, I think. It should allow any wizard or sorcerer to cast more first and second level spells."

"Obviously, I should take that." Master White held out his soft palm expectantly. "Since you don't use combat spells."

"If I keep it," she pointed out, "then I'd be able to cast utility spells like see invisibility. It would give me a lot more flexibility, and I'd still be able to buff the party."

"Give me the ring, Kit." Master White folded his arms, and eyed her like she were a misbehaving child. "Or do you think it's worth a party vote?"

"Fine." Her shoulders slumped. She was so tired of fighting over everything, and even if she won the vote she'd never hear the end of it. "Here. Take it." She handed it across, and Master White slid the ring on his finger with a contented sigh. Right next to the other ring, and the bracelets, and the amulet, and the robes that the party had let him loot.

"Can I have the shield?" Brakestuff asked, presenting the shining silver buckler. "It's the same AC, but I'd have less armor check penalty so I wouldn't suck so badly at sneaking."

"Very well," Master White waved magnanimously. "You can buy it from the party, and we'll even give you a 20% discount."

"Awesome." Brakestuff removed his old shield, a heavy, steel kite shield, and dumped it on the ground next to him. He clipped on the buckler, then used it to reflect sunlight into Crotchshot's eyes. "This thing is going to make hiking so much less boring."

"Oww! If you do that again you'd better make sure you're wearing a cup," the elf snapped as he reached threateningly for his quiver.

Kit lost interest in their antics, and took a quick look at the cave. Piles of coins still dotted the cave, but it was all copper, which no self-respecting adventurer would stoop to gathering. It was too heavy, and a single gold was worth a hundred copper. Silver was heavy, but still worth enough that they usually took it too.

She made one final inspection of the cave, just in case, but there were no secret entrances, or if there were she'd missed her perception check. She gave a weary sigh and exited the cave. Once again she'd come away with nothing, while Master White got the best loot.

A wall of particularly foul stench greeted her as she exited the cave. It was coming from the dragon's corpse, which had continued to decay at a supernatural rate while they'd been pillaging its lair. Its scales had gone a dusty grey, and its eyes were now cloudy and unfocused.

Then the dragon began climbing to its feet.

"Guys!" Kit shouted, as she stumbled back a pace. "I don't think the dragon is dead."

"Oh, it's dead," Master White crowed as he walked by her. "Or undead rather. I animated it."

"What possible use could you have for an undead dragon?" she demanded, glaring at the necromancer in horror. "I thought your alignment was lawful good."

"It is." He blinked at her in confusion. "And I resent you implying otherwise. This isn't an evil act. It's expediency."

"What do you mean?"

"We're going to use the dragon to fly out of here. It will shave hours off the trip."

"Uh, I don't know about that," Crotchshot protested. The elf led his horse past the undead dragon, and the creature whinnied in terror, the whites of its eyes flashing. "Crap, horse. Calm down. It ain't gonna hurt you." He looked up at

White. "I ain't gonna leave my horse behind. That's crazy talk. This thing is worth fifty gold, and I'm broke. I could get like five whores for a whole night if we sell it."

"We just looted nearly six thousand gold, by my count." White smiled magnanimously. "The time is more valuable. If we get back we'll have time to resupply, level up, and then hit the Tomb of Deadly Death before the dark lord even knows we're in his city." The necromancer turned to Brakestuff, who was using his new shield to blind the horses. "What do you think, my short, stupid friend?"

"Hmm?" The dwarf looked up, and pushed a mop of hair from his face so he could see the necromancer. "Oh, about the dragon thing? My god is pretty clear. Knowsbest has decreed that the righteous shall prevail. Righteous means good, right? What's your alignment, Master White?"

"Lawful good, of course." Master White smiled triumphantly at Kit. "Crotchshot, did I mention that this dragon has a base fly speed of ninety?"

"Ninety?" Crotchshot blinked at the undead wyrm. "Shit, why are we still using horses?" He slid off his mount, and withdrew his saddlebags.

"You're just going to leave your mount here, in the heart of a deadly forest?" Kit gawked at Crotchshot. "Every time I think you can't do something lower, you prove me wrong. You're supposed to be a ranger. You can't just abandon your horse."

"I'm not abandoning it." The elf slung his pack over his shoulder and moved to stand next to the animated dragon. "I'm setting it free. It's, uh, magnanimous. Nature and stuff. I mean, if you think it would make sense, I guess I could put it out of its misery." He reached for an arrow.

Kit recoiled. "By shooting it in the dick?"

"It's a gelding, but that general area, yeah."

"That doesn't mean what you think it means. Geldings still have a—you know what? Never mind. I'm sure the horse would rather take its chances." Kit shuddered, and took a few steps away from the corpse the others were clambering on top of. She tried not to focus on the wide stand of now-dead trees that had been killed by the necromancer. Everywhere they went they seemed to leave the world a worse place, which hardly fit the necromancer's stated alignment.

"Well then," Master White said as he climbed atop the dragon. "I guess we'll see you back in town, Kit. I'll hold onto your share of the treasure for you until then."

The dragon kicked off the ground, and began soaring into the air. Rancid blood dripped from the hideous wounds they'd inflicted, and the stench was a living thing as the beast lifted off and winged its way above the trees.

Kit reached for her magic and shifted into her natural form, a small, red fox. She sprinted into the trees, working her way through the valley as the dragon sped by overhead. It was worth a couple extra days not to have to smell that thing the entire trip back.

3

THREE WHOLE SILVER

Bert crept down into the valley, as quickly as his stubby legs would allow. He wound past pine cones, roots, and rocks, and finally reached level ground. The adventurers were emerging from the cave, and had approached the corpse of the dragon they'd slain.

To Bert's immense surprise, the dragon stood up again. Bert immediately backpedaled, then dropped into a fetal position behind a large rock. Probably not large enough to save him. He lay there quivering for several long moments before he raised the courage to open an eye.

The dragon hadn't used its breath weapon, but if it did he didn't even get a saving throw. Any amount of area damage was pretty much instant death.

Thankfully, the adventurers were using the dragon as a mount, and its head was now facing away from Bert. He felt much better.

Bert courageously rose from behind the rock, and stealthily made his way inside the cave. He probably should have waited for the adventurers to leave, but they'd never noticed him before.

This time, though, one of their number had stayed behind. The sorceress stood there in her enchanted finery, turning in a slow circle as she surveyed the forest.

The dragon leapt into the air with the rest of her party, leaving the sorceress behind. Bert wondered why, and hoped that she wasn't guarding the cave for some reason. He hurried inside, and had almost made it when the sorceress turned into a fox.

Bert paused to watch. Her whole body shrank and rippled, and then the elf was gone and in her place sat a bright-red fox. He'd seen the trick before, and it made her the perfect-sized mount for someone his size. If only. She sprinted off into the trees, and he gave a longing sigh as he watched her go. With a mount like that he could get his first full-hit die. Maybe even two someday. If he rolled well he could have like twelve hit points.

Bert turned back to the cave's shadowed interior. The trove wasn't going to loot itself. Bert carried his pack inside, and set it against the far wall. He withdrew his most prized invention, a rake with a collapsible handle that he'd assembled from a spring and an old broom.

He set to work with a will, and began raking out the piles of copper. It took long minutes, but when he was done he'd evened out the piles into a thick carpet of metal across the entire floor. Once he was done, Bert hurried over to his pack, and withdrew his flint and tinder, then shoved his arm into his pack, and pulled out a torch.

Bert lit the torch, and began walking slowly back and forth across the cave. He searched diligently, kneeling whenever he saw a glint that might be silver or gold. The process was slow, but profitable. It took Bert until the torch had burned down to a third of its length, but by that time he'd found three whole silver.

He shoved the much more valuable coins into his loin-cloth, and then began gathering as much copper as he could carry into his pack. That was about twice as many as his fingers and toes combined. More was tempting, but the hills were tall, and he was just a tiny goblin.

Bert exited the cave, and hummed to himself as he retraced his steps back up the ridge. This was his fourth adventure, and this haul was by far the most profitable. He had almost four hundred copper now. It seemed like so much.

He wondered how much a mount would cost. Bert had never been inside the human city, but he'd seen the monster shop from outside. They sold dire wolves. If he could buy one of those then he'd finally be promoted to warg rider, and then he'd be respected.

Bert quickened his pace, and reached the top of the ridge before he knew it. He hurried down the far side, and took the most direct route towards his home, the town of Paradise.

The neighboring valley was full of monsters, most of which he'd seen on the way in. He passed an x-clops, the nastier cousin of the traditional cyclops. This one was taller and still only had one eye, but unlike a regular cyclops it could fire a ruby eye beam that incinerated targets. It was pretty easy to tell the types apart, as the x-clops wore a blue and gold suit instead of the usual dirty loincloth.

Bert walked directly between the x-clops's feet, and the giant ignored him, just like it ignored all the other critters scattered around the valley. He threaded through the valley, the sun sinking lower in the sky as he made it to the far side.

He passed a group of well-endowed centaurs, who were always humping things, but fortunately they couldn't see him. Bert didn't want to be on the receiving end of a centaur. No one did.

He'd nearly reached the top of the next ridge when Bert almost walked into a group of endless ents. He froze, and backed slowly away from the large, black oak trees. They were much more dangerous than they appeared. Endless ents never stopped talking, and once one started the rest would surround you and start peppering you with questions.

Bert had heard stories of people getting trapped in their moots, and dying of starvation. He didn't know if it was true, but Bert circled wide around the trees, careful to stay out of their reach as he toddled past, the weight of his pack causing him to sway with every step.

Finally, Bert made it to the top of the far ridge, on the opposite side of the valley. He wearily set his pack against a rock, and began unrolling his tent. Below him, in the next valley, he could see the glimmering lights of Paradise.

The sun was low in the sky, but he could probably make it before dark, if he wanted. Did he?

Bert shook his head, then dumped his coins in the dirt and started to count them. He liked counting. It was easy out here, alone, where he could think.

Tomorrow he'd have to go home though, and there were so many goblins. It made thinking difficult, and he hated it. He couldn't even read when he was around too many goblins, and he lost so many words.

Bert finished counting with a contented sigh, and added the last copper back to his pack. This had to be enough. Soon, he'd be a warg rider.

Bert would be important.

4

PARADISE

Bert woke up before the sun, and his teeth chattered as he slipped out of his bedroll. He rubbed at his arms, which had gone a much lighter shade of green than normal. Breaking down his campsite kept him moving, which warmed him up.

He finished tying his bedroll, then attached it to his pack. Bert decided to eat as he walked, and withdrew a small bag of mushrooms he'd gathered the day before. He scarfed them down as he started down the switchbacks into the valley below.

It descended for nearly two miles before reaching the valley floor, where Paradise lay. He could see the village from up here, with small, checkered farms bordering the dump itself. Dozens of haphazard houses had been constructed from the garbage humans dumped over the cliffs, and the town had earned its name when the first goblin realized that the humans brought another offering of garbage every week, like clockwork.

Bert thought it strange that the humans would go

through the trouble to send them offerings, as the goblins were no threat. The idea became less odd as he picked his way down the ridge. Thinking became harder. Big words became scary.

He hated the feeling, which smothered all his ideas for various inventions. Bert sighed and continued down the path, once again considering moving out of the village and into a cave somewhere. He really was happier alone, most of the time.

But if he did that then there would be no one to watch over his mother.

Bert redoubled his pace when he reached the valley floor, and waddled up the path toward the residential side of the village. A few of the goblins working in the farms looked up at him, but no one waved or called out in greeting. It wasn't that they disliked him, but the village was small and most people had learned that Bert cared about very different things than they did.

"Bert!" a guttural voice barked from behind him. It was accompanied by the low growl of a warg.

He froze.

"You trying to sneak in with treasure?" Head Warg Rider demanded. The much bigger goblin's warg trotted closer, its hot breath almost making Bert gag. He held a spear, with a wicked-looking tip.

"Bert not sneaking." Bert unslung his pack, and reluctantly dumped the contents into the dirt. "Head Warg Rider can take cut."

Bert avoided looking at Head Warg Rider. He'd bullied Bert back when he'd been a warg rider, and would love to take something valuable from Bert, but Head Warg Rider also didn't understand that humans used copper as a form of currency.

"More bits of metal." Head Warg Rider picked up a copper and peered at it. "Ain't even shiny. Why collect these things for?"

Bert opened his mouth to explain his plan. He was going to...what was he going to do again? Thinking was hard. Oh yeah. "Bert buy mount with it."

Head Warg Rider blinked at him, and then started to laugh. The warg started laughing too. So did a few of the nearby goblins, working the rows of corn lining the road.

"How Bert do that?" Head Warg Rider wheezed in between laughs. "Nobody want stupid metal."

Bert's mind was hazy, but he still remembered enough of the plan. "Humies trade for it. Bert go to humie town, and buy warg."

Head Warg Rider clutched at his side laughing, and tears carved paths in the dirt coating his cheeks as he doubled over. He shook his head at Bert, and rode off in the opposite direction.

Bert calmly stuffed his copper into his pack, and slipped the straps over his shoulders, then started waddling up the path again. Head Warg Rider kept laughing as Bert walked away, but at least he didn't try to take any of Bert's copper. Putting the silver in his loincloth had been smart. Those Head Warg Rider might have taken. Silver was shiny.

He entered the outskirts of Paradise, which smelled of rotten eggs and burnt rubber, mostly. A miasma of various odors gathered here, baked by the summer sun until it reached what his mother called a soupy smell.

Bert hurried past a couple more warg riders, and doffed his little cap when he passed G. Mayor, the leader of their village. G. Mayor eyed Bert with disapproval, but was deep in conversation with his chief garbologist, thankfully. Bert kept his head down and waddled up the lane, where his mother's warren lay.

Those towering garbage stacks were all Bert had ever known. He'd been born into the unstable towers, though there had only been two stories when he'd been very young. Now there were three, every room of it both constructed and packed with scavenged junk.

Bert's pace slowed as he approached. He didn't want to go inside. Going inside meant talking to his mother, and she'd have nothing kind to say. He stopped entirely, and briefly considered going straight to the human settlement. No, he needed to stop home long enough to pick up the rest of his treasure.

He prepared himself to be humiliated, and waddled toward the closest entrance to his mother's warren. Several warg pups were playing outside, chasing and yapping, and occasionally belching out clouds of frost. Bert patted his legs and tried to call one over, but the pups ignored him.

He hung his shoulders again, and crawled inside the garbage tunnel.

"Berrrrt!" His mother's shrill voice echoed down the tunnel, as if she'd sensed the exact instant he entered, like a spider feeling its web being strummed.

He winced, and then wormed his way up the garbage tunnel. He had to move carefully, and avoided a bent nail that had caught his shin more than once. Bert scaled the rickety ladder leading to the second level, and managed to grab the rail at the top before the weight of his pack pulled him back the way he'd come.

He rested a moment, then headed up the tunnel to the living room, where his mother spent most of her time. He tumbled down a slope of garbage, and landed in a heap next to his mother's enormous cushion, where she sat sorting garbage.

She wore a badly scuffed top hat, which she hadn't been wearing when he left. "Bert bring stuff?" His mother studied him, and her gaze settled on his pack. She leaned forward and her eyes narrowed when he didn't answer. "Bert find good garbage out there? Or waste more time?"

"Bert not find much," he admitted. Bert dumped his copper out for what he hoped would be the last time today. "Just more metal." He stared down at the dizzying number of coins, and wished he could summon the numbers to count them. It was just so hard to think around other goblins.

"Why Bert waste time?" She frowned down at the metal, and kicked a coin into the wall. "Bert could have lots of garbage. Bert waste so much time. Bert never find anything interesting."

"Don't want Bert's copper?"

"Course not," she snarled, glaring at him. "Go away."

Bert collected his copper with a sigh, and carried his pack up to his room. Getting there required him to crawl though the tunnel he'd burrowed in his mother's garbage, which was always shifting and changing. He wormed his way through, and finally tugged his pack inside the little cubby that had been given to him when he was a baby. It was just large enough for him and his pack.

There wasn't enough room for a mount, he realized. If he did get a warg where would it live? Maybe he could clear out some garbage. Or maybe he'd finally start building his own warren.

Bert slowly removed his copper, one by one, and added them to a broken flower pot he'd found a few weeks back. The metal filled it almost to the brim, but he couldn't count it to know how much he had. Most of that metal had been rolled into tubes of twenty copper each, but he was too tired to do the same for the new coins he'd brought.

Hopefully, it was enough. Tomorrow he could head to the human village, and trade all the bits of metal for his very own mount.

5

$PLACEHOLDER

Bert's head was muddy when he woke up. He spent several minutes rummaging through the garbage coating his floor, which produced a piece of old bread that could have been mistaken for concrete. Mmm, breakfast.

By the time he'd found some water to soak it in, Bert remembered. Today was the day. He was going somewhere no other goblin had ever gone. The human town of $Placeholder. He didn't know what to expect, really, as he'd only seen it from the ridge outside. But they sold wargs, and he had money.

He stuffed the uneaten hunk of the bread into his pack, and slung it over his shoulder, then wormed his way through garbage tunnels until he reached his mother's living room. She eyed him noncommittally as he slunk past her, and didn't speak until he'd made it to the doorway.

"Bert going out for more pieces of stupid metal?" Her tone made it very clear what she thought of that. "Past time Bert think about adding to warren. Bert should have tunnels, and a lady friend to give Bert a litter. Bert last one still at home."

"Bert will bring back good junk," Bert promised, then hurried out before she could respond. He waddled down the lane, hurrying away from her house as fast as a tiny goblin could manage.

It was so hard to think. He kept feeling like there was an idea he'd forgotten, but when he searched, he ended up chasing his tail, like a warg pup. All he knew is that he had to get out of Paradise and into the wild. Then he'd be able to think.

The sunlight had just begun to crest the mountains to the east, but hadn't filtered down into the valley yet. It was still dark, and almost everyone was asleep. Just like he liked it. There were no warg riders to harass him, and no G. Mayor to judge him. It was just him and the trees, and after today it would be him, the trees, and his awesome new warg.

Bert picked a slow path up the mountains on the opposite side of the valley from Paradise, the ones that led toward the human kingdoms. By the time he made it to the top of the ridge, the sun was high in the sky. His legs were wobbly, and he was fairly certain someone had added several large rocks to his pack.

He found a shady spot off the path where he could peer down at $Placeholder, the furthest edge of the human kingdom. From what little he'd learned following adventurers, it was the last town they'd built before their kingdom went into decline.

Little plumes of smoke rose from rectangular buildings, most squat and low to the ground. Here and there an inn might rise to three stories, but it was as if nothing were allowed to compete with the mausoleum perched atop the highest hill in town.

The black stone edifice sat there, silent and foreboding, the dark stones piled almost as high as the mountains surrounding the valley.

"The Tomb of Deadly Death," Bert muttered, staring in awe as he removed his pack. He stretched, and started unlimbering his tiny arms.

Setting down the pack relieved him more than it usually had. He should have considered that carrying all of his money at once would be hard. At least he'd only have to do it once.

He inhaled deeply, and smiled down at $Placeholder. He only had one more task to do before he could walk into town. He reached into his pack and withdrew several sleeves of paper he'd made from scraps at the dump. Each had been designed to hold twenty copper, and held them in a single rolled tube. It made counting and carrying them much easier.

Bert hummed to himself as he filled the last three tubes, and sealed them with a nearly empty jar of glue he'd found in the dump last month. He proudly returned them all to his pack, picked it up, and started down the hillside toward $Placeholder.

Logically he knew that entering the town was safe. The citizens ignored critters, just like adventurers did, and most monsters. But there were so many scary new things. Loud wagons rumbled down narrow cobblestone streets. Horses whinnied, so tall and stinky. A casual step from one of those legs could crush him.

Bert threaded through the late afternoon traffic filtering into the town. Getting in required you to cross a bridge, which was guarded by a pair of skeletal knights. They stood at attention in their dark armor at either side of the gate leading into the city, while a trio of ratlings with clipboards interrogated those entering.

Bert listened to their questions, which mostly concerned what they were bringing into the city, and how much it was worth. The people they were talking to would reluctantly get out coins, most of them silver, and a few gold, and dejectedly hand them to the ratlings.

Momentary vindication surged through him. They *were* using coins. The coins were valuable, just like he'd always tried to tell everyone.

But vindication, one of the largest words he knew, was quickly overpowered by one of the smallest. Fear. The rats would want to take some of Bert's coins.

He dropped prone against the ground, and began shimmying away from the line, toward the stone wall behind the skeletal guard. He risked a quick glance around, and saw several other critters. There were a few ravens, a squirrel, and a single moat slug.

The ravens ignored him, as ravens tended to do. They were smug birds, which Bert supposed made sense. If he were a cool-looking bird, and he could fly, he'd probably feel pretty smug too.

Bert waddled past the moat slug, who eyed him curiously with one of its two eyestalks.

"Where are you going?" the slug asked. It oozed a little bit closer, but it was even slower than Bert.

"Bert here to shop," he explained. Then Bert hesitated. Could he trust this slug? What if it tried to rob him? He could probably just walk away, but caution seemed smart. "Bert want to buy mount."

The slug blinked up at him. "Oh, well, will you be passing back by this way?"

Bert shrugged, and looked around. He took a deep

breath, and realized his head felt much clearer than he had even this morning. "Probably. Bert need to go home after, so come by here."

The slug oozed a little closer, and Bert took a step back to match. "I realize we've only just met, but if you're willing to procure something for me, then I'm willing to trade some valuable information."

"What information slug need?" Bert's curiosity was aroused. The slug could be well connected. Most slugs were. Or probably were. Bert had never actually met one.

"I know a secret way into the Tomb of Deadly Death." The slug seemed quite proud of the information.

"Hmm." Bert considered the offer. That sounded very valuable, although he'd probably not go someplace so dangerous himself. There would be many monsters with area-of-effect attacks, making it a lethal place for a 1-HP critter. "What Bert need to procure?"

He liked that word. It sounded much fancier than get.

"All that grows around here is lichen," the slug explained. It waved an eyestalk at a patch of green on the base of the castle wall. "I'm not allowed to leave my post. If you can bring me some mushrooms, or strawberries, or even some carrion—not too old, mind—then I'll tell you everything I know about the tomb."

"Okay." Bert removed his pack, and withdrew his note pad.

Momentary anxiety gripped him as he fished out his charcoal, but thankfully he'd been away from Paradise long enough to draw a picture of the slug, a plus sign, some mushrooms and strawberries, and then an equal sign with his best attempt at the tomb. It was really just a square house with a frownie face on it. Close enough.

"Bert will help." Bert replaced his writing tools, and picked up his pack. "Be back soon."

He hurried over to the wall, terrified that the ratlings would see him. They weren't critters, and apparently had NPC class levels, as evidenced by their ability to read and write.

Fortunately, all three seemed focused on fleecing their current targets. Bert hurried past them, huddling against the wall as he snuck through and into the city.

A wall of noise and smells washed over him, nearly all of them unfamiliar. Bert's eyes widened, and he briefly regretted coming.

$Placeholder was scary.

6

BOBERTON

Bert summoned his courage and started up the cobblestone street. He dodged a wagon wheel, and then leapt out of the way of a farm wife carrying three squirming chickens. A pile of horse dung splashed into the street ahead of him, but he twisted nimbly around it and managed to avoid getting any on his shoes.

Navigating the obstacle course was exhausting, especially with his heavy pack. Bert was soon coated in sweat, but he refused to give up or take a break. He reminded himself that doing this on the way back wouldn't be necessary, because he'd have an awesome new mount.

Bert climbed atop a discarded crate at the mouth of an alley, and stood on his tiptoes. He'd made it about halfway down the street, and if his view from the ridge over town was accurate, the monster shop should be right around the corner.

He clambered down from the box, and started back through the crowd. By the time he reached the corner his chest was heaving, and his legs were wobbling even worse than when he'd climbed the mountain the day before.

Maybe there was a reason adventurers never picked up copper.

Bert gave himself several moments to catch his breath, then slunk around the corner and started up the new street. This one wasn't as wide, but there also wasn't nearly as much traffic. A window on the second floor of a nearby building opened, and a woman leaned out to dump a bucket of slop.

Filth rained down on Bert, splattering him, his pack, and the cobblestones around him. He sighed, and wished for longer legs. Being a goblin was not easy.

He resolutely continued. His warg was waiting. Bert pushed up the street, and passed three more buildings before seeing a sign with a baby gold dragon, and three dollar signs underneath.

Bert found a hidden reserve of energy, and ran the final ten feet to the door. He'd made it! Finally, he was going to get his mount. He peered up at the door, and realized that the handle was out of reach.

"Hmm," he mused, studying the outside of the building. Both windows were closed.

He studied the door handle, which wasn't that far out of reach. Bert removed his pack and propped it against the door, then clambered atop the pack, until he was high enough to reach the handle. He leaned hard against it, and the door opened suddenly, spilling Bert and his pack inside.

"Hmm?" came from a bespectacled man behind the counter. He had wispy grey hair, and a grey hat to match.

The man peered down at the open door, but didn't seem to see Bert. He ambled over, and picked up Bert's pack, his free hand supporting the small of his back. "That's odd. Did someone drop it off, I wonder? Why? The straps are too small for an adult. A child then? How strange."

Bert panicked. He couldn't lose all his money. It was unlikely he could take this guy in a fight, but he had to try. Bert charged. He ran straight at the man's leg, and jumped high enough to punch the knee with all his might.

"Hmm?" The man adjusted his spectacles, and peered down in Bert's direction. "Oh my. Are you...a goblin? This must belong to you then." He handed Bert his pack, and Bert quickly strapped it back on. The man gave him a friendly smile. "Can't say I've ever seen a goblin before. Are you here to purchase a monster then?"

Bert nodded eagerly.

"Excellent, excellent. Please, come inside." The man held the door for Bert, and closed it in his wake. He strode magnanimously to the counter, and pulled over a chair that made it much easier for Bert to clamber up and see over the counter. The man waited until Bert had settled, and then moved behind the counter and gave another friendly smile. Bert liked him immediately. "What are you in the market for, young feller? A G. Scorpion, maybe? Nah, that doesn't seem your style. How about a griffin then? You could soar over everyone, and I've trained it to poop on command. It's great for dealing with enemies, without getting arrested. Come to think of it, I'm keeping the griffin. But I've got plenty of other creatures for sale. What's your pleasure, son?"

"Bert want warg," he explained. He did his best imitation, extending his hands as claws and exposing his teeth. "Grr, like wolf, but breathe frost."

"Ahh, I've got just the thing." The man rubbed his hands together. "I've got a dire wolf, son. It's a little bigger than your average warg, but if you're looking to get some respect when you saunter through town, that's the mount for you. You live up at Paradise then?"

"Yup." Bert nodded absently as he dug into his pack. He started getting out tubes of coppers as fast as he could manage, and began stacking them up on the counter. "Bert have lots of coin. How much warg cost? You tell Bert when to stop getting out coins."

Bert kept adding rolls. Each time he reached into the pack he had to reach a little deeper, and began to worry as he had fewer and fewer to pull out. The man still hadn't asked him to stop, and was now eyeing him with a strange expression he'd never seen before.

"Uh, let me stop you right there, son." His tone was grave, and held the kind of respect Bert usually only saw used when G. Mayor gave speeches.

Bert's eyes widened as he remembered his secret weapon. He shoved a hand down his loincloth, and emerged with all three silver, which he slapped down on the counter next to the rolls of copper. "That enough?"

"Son, a dire wolf will run you four hundred gold pieces." The old man placed a comforting hand on Bert's shoulder. "Your amount of coin might get you one of the basic pets. Now that ain't a mount, but it does mean leaving here with a new friend. And from the look of you I think you could use a friend."

Hmm, Bert thought. The shopkeeper was right. He did like the idea of having a friend. But, it hurt to know he couldn't afford the dire wolf. "How much more gold Bert need for dire wolf?"

"Three hundred and ninety-four," the man supplied. "In fact, if you can come up with half the money, I'll give you a discount. Two hundred GP will get you your mount. You find a way to do that, son, and I will be damned impressed."

"Okay." Bert stared at his coins on the counter. He really didn't want to carry it all the way back, and if he was being honest with himself, he had to admit his mom was right. Copper wasn't really worth it, even to a goblin. So he may as well spend it, and then come up with another way to get gold.

He stared up at the shopkeeper. "Can Bert see pets?"

"Of course." The man came out from behind the counter, and started up a narrow hallway. "Right this way, son."

The man led Bert into a small room with a half dozen animal cages. All of them were full, each with a creature that was roughly Bert-sized, and therefore unsuitable to use as a mount.

Bert passed by each cage in turn, and paused in front of a large, white chicken. It was almost big enough. Maybe he could make it work.

Before deciding, he wanted to see his other options, though. Bert continued up the line of cages, and stopped in front of the next interesting one. It contained a large tortoise, easily big enough for Bert to sit on. The tortoise eyed him sleepily. Unfortunately, it would be a very, very slow mount.

The last cage held the most promise. It contained a large bulldog pup, with reddish skin, that was easily as tall as Bert. He peered up at the man. "Why dog have two heads?"

"That's a mutant demo pup," the shopkeeper explained. He squatted down next to the cage. "You see how one of the heads is asleep right now? It has a completely different personality from the other one. So it's almost like you're getting two pets for the price of one."

The dog pranced over to the edge of its cage, and the head that was awake started to sniff Bert's hand. The creature had a large nose, and big, soulful eyes.

A long, low fart split the room, and Bert's eyes began to burn. Even the dog whined, and wagged its stubby tail.

Bert waved at the air in front of his face, and after a moment the stench cleared. He could learn to live with that, if that was the only drawback. He studied the dog, who was a little taller than him, now that it was standing. It wasn't quite big enough to ride.

"Will dog grow?" Bert folded his arms, and tried to look intimidating. His mother told him that shopkeepers gave bad deals if they didn't fear you.

"Quite a bit, son." The man opened the cage, and the demo pup cautiously emerged. "You give Boberton here a steady supply of magic pellets and he'll never really stop growing. He's likely to outlive you, too, and he'll be pretty good sized by the time you're a goblin elder."

"Why his name bobe-err-ton?" Bert demanded.

"It was randomly generated, like all pets." The man held up his hands helplessly. "Unfortunately, they can't be changed. I wish they could, but I don't make the rules."

"Okay," Bert decided aloud. "Bert will take Boberton. Throw in pellets too?"

"Why not?" The shopkeeper gave another weathered smile.

The dog seemed to like Bert, and eventually he could use it as a mount. If the shopkeeper was telling the truth, he might be even bigger than a warg some day. Bert closed his eyes so he could use his imagination, and envisioned a Boberton the size of a house. Bert smiled.

He opened his eyes when the dog started licking him. "Oh. Dog very friendly."

"Only to you." The shopkeeper handed Bert a leash, then connected the other end to Boberton's collar. "Now that you've purchased him he'll show up in your inventory, and he'll obey only your commands. You make sure you keep him fed, son, or he'll start to get real mean."

"What dog eat if run out of pellets?" Bert hoped whatever it was wasn't too expensive.

"Boberton will eat anything, really. He's not gonna like fruit too much, but you give him meat, grains, that sort of thing, and he'll be one happy dog." The man patted Bert on the head, which Bert kind of liked. "Enjoy your new friend, son. If you ever come up with that gold you come back, and we'll see about that warg."

Bert accepted the leash from the shopkeeper, and led his new friend out into the city. He couldn't be happier.

7

NEGATIVE QUALITY

K it was exhausted by the time she trotted into $Placeholder, but had also enjoyed the run as it gave her time to think. Besides, being in fox form never got old. She loved bounding through the forest, and sampling the tapestry of scents her vulpine form afforded.

When she reached the bridge leading into town Kit reluctantly shifted back into elven form. Her staff and robes clearly identified her as a sorceress, and most travelers kept their distance as she moved to join the back of the line.

She stared up at the Tomb of Deadly Death, its foreboding stone looming over everyone. That place was designed to be scary, and despite White's assurances that it would be easy, she had her doubts. No one took a dark lord down easy.

"What are you declaring?" A ratling demanded as it scurried up her leg, then her midsection, and finally clambered onto the pack.

"Nothing." And she wasn't lying. She had the same gear she'd left with, since White had taken all the loot from the dragon. He'd probably flown over the wall, too, which might have meant he avoided customs.

The ratling spent a few moments rummaging through her pack, but gave up when it found nothing it could tax. "Fine. You're free to go." It leapt off her, and onto the next person in line.

Kit started up the main thoroughfare, and made for the inn where they often stayed. She passed the usual foot traffic, but noticed that there were more skeletal guards than usual. Something had happened to put up the dark lord's guard, and that wasn't good.

She redoubled her pace and made for the inn. None of the skeletons accosted her, but she still didn't like their empty gazes. They were a visible reminder that a much more powerful necromancer existed in the city, one that could probably trounce White in a fair fight. Which is why it was her job to help make sure that fight was anything but fair.

It didn't take long to reach the inn, the Salty Gamer. White had made the place impossible to miss, as he'd parked the newly animated dragon directly outside, where horses were normally tethered.

The few frightened beasts were huddled as far as they could get from the undead dragon, which seemed not to care about their presence. The stench finally reached her as she neared the doors, and she found herself coughing. That thing was even more rank in the close confines of the surrounding buildings.

She escaped into the inn. The grime-stained door opened with a creak, and she sighed contentedly as she stepped out of the stench and into a wall of heat, both from bodies and from the fire roaring in the hearth. One other advantage of fox form was fur, and she found herself growing cold easily in elven form.

Brakestuff's raucous laugh came from the far side of the room, where her companions had commandeered the largest table. Empty plates with discarded bones and small puddles of gravy sat before them, along with a dozen or more empty tankards.

She picked a path through the crowd, and slid into the empty chair next to Crotchshot, as far from White as she could get.

"Ah, Kit," he said, tone magnanimous, "you've finally arrived. We've only been here for three hours or so." White leaned closer, and the firelight painted his features with a sinister brush, especially the goatee. "We avoided customs, which saved us twelve hundred gold. Plus, we were able to get training credit while we were flying. You can't do that on a horse, or in fox form. Guess you must feel pretty stupid, huh?"

"You have no idea." White missed the irony, of course. She raised a hand and flagged down a barmaid. The woman quickly hurried over, and seemed relieved that she didn't have to flirt.

"What'll you have?" The woman held a tray with several empty mugs, and didn't seem to need a pad to record orders.

"Wine. Anything white is good. If you don't have that, then a soft red." She knew it was unlikely to find something decent to drink in a place that specialized in cheap ale, but she'd been surprised on more than one adventure.

"I'll fetch you something nice." She bobbed a curtsy, and hurried back toward the kitchen.

Kit turned her attention to the drunken conversation, and noted how flushed Crotchshot was. Six of the empty tankards sat before him, and he didn't have the body weight to deal with that much ale.

"I'm gonna spend my XP on improved initiative," he slurred, sipping at a mug before continuing, "that'll bring me up to a +12. I like making things dead before they get to go." No one seemed especially interested, so Crotchshot turned to White. "How about you, White? What are you spending your XP on?"

The necromancer dabbed at his chin with a napkin, and then set it primly next to him, as if unaware of how it contrasted with his stained robes. "I believe I'm going to buy off a negative quality."

Kit cocked her head at that. It was rare for someone to buy off a negative quality, as most people selected flaws that were easy to play around, and thus flaws in name only. Crotchshot's 'curse' was a great example. Buying one off generally indicated a mistake in character creation, and that didn't sound at all like White.

Brakestuff looked up from the chicken he'd been devouring. Much of it had migrated to his beard. "Which negative quality?"

"My family," White answered smoothly. He gave a frustrated shake of his head. "I really underestimated how much of a penalty they'd be to training time."

"Wait," Kit demanded. Everyone turned to face her, and most seemed surprised she'd spoken. "Are you telling me that you're divorcing your wife and abandoning your child because you want to spend more hours training?"

White eyed her with something between contempt and disbelief that the benefits of that solution weren't immediately apparent to her. "Of course not. I'm not divorcing her. I just won't have to spend any time with her now. Before, I had to spend one hour with my family for every hour I spent training. Do you have any idea how tedious that is?"

"Hey!" Crotchshot perked up. "Can't you just take the deadbeat dad negative quality, and spend the experience on a spell or something?"

White seemed to consider that for a long while. "No, I don't want the social penalties that come with the deadbeat dad quality. That would mean less money when vendoring gear." He nodded, as if he'd finally convinced himself. "Yeah, buying off the family quality is the way to go. I'm at a point where it's really hindering how many spells I can learn."

Crotchshot nodded sympathetically, while Brakestuff had gone back to devouring his chicken. These were the people she was trying to save the world with. A fictional world, maybe, but one she was trying to pretend was real. Wasn't that the whole point of roleplaying?

White scooted out from behind the table, and stretched. He covered a yawn. "I'm going to go speak with the shop-keeper to see if they've sold the gear we left. I'll bring every-one's share back, and we can go shopping in the morning. After that, it's time to head into the tomb. Don't get too drunk, and be ready to go at dawn."

Kit nodded, though she wasn't sure either of the others heard. She had a bad feeling about their trip into the tomb, but there wasn't anything she could do right now.

The barmaid came back and deposited a wooden mug with a clear, sweet-smelling liquid. "Brought you some mead. It's the best we have. Hope that suits." She gave a gap-toothed smile, and gratefully accepted the silver Kit gave her.

Kit resolved to spend the rest of the evening enjoying herself. Tomorrow they were back on the clock.

8

ONE MAN'S TRASH

Bert left the monster shop in high spirits, despite not being able to afford a mount. Boberton trotted dutifully after him, and the demo pup seemed pleased to be with Bert. Well, half of him did anyway. The left head, which he decided to call Lefty, was friendly and obedient. The right one, on the other hand, or other head rather, growled whenever he approached.

Bert made sure to walk next to Lefty as he led Boberton up the street. It was a little easier now, because as a pet Boberton was more visible than Bert. Pets had hit points, and both adventurers and townspeople could see them.

They made their way up and down several streets, and the walking was much, much more enjoyable now that he wasn't burdened with all that copper. Bert's pack felt extra light, and he laughed as he leapt over puddles. Boberton didn't seem to get the concept, and walked right through them, leaving a trail of large, muddy paw prints.

Bert navigated unerringly toward the inn where the adventurers would be staying. They were, thankfully, creatures of habit and had stayed there every time he'd observed from his perch on the ridge over town.

Finding the building in the city was a little harder than seeing it from above, but Bert was feeling more and more clearheaded, and eventually he saw a temple that he recognized. A giant statue of a man pointing at himself with both thumbs while he smiled at the onlooker sat atop a three-story, white building.

Several skeletons stood outside, each holding a pike twice as long as they were tall, and the temple seemed to be abandoned, or at least hadn't been used in a very long time. The inn the party stayed at was right across the street.

Bert waddled across the cobblestones, and perked up when he saw the undead dragon lounging outside. "This right place. Bert smart."

He considered going inside, but Boberton would complicate that now. Instead, he wandered over to an alley next to the inn, and peered carefully down it. The cobblestones were covered in grime, but were depressingly devoid of usable refuse. However, there was a garbage can right next to the back door, and a quick whiff told him someone had recently discarded chicken in there.

Bert patted Lefty. "Boberton, want to try some real meat?"

Lefty stood at attention, the big dog's tiny ears going fully erect as he panted. He nudged Righty, who woke up with a snort.

Bert carefully removed the lid to the garbage can, and clambered up the side. He landed atop a pile of crumpled paper, which smelled wonderful. Bert rummaged inside, and was shocked to discover four fully intact chicken legs. They'd been cooked in some sort of spice, and he began to salivate.

Bert peered suspiciously around the garbage can, but it wasn't a trap. Someone had intentionally discarded this food. It made no sense.

He carefully bundled up the paper, and hopped out of the garbage can. Lefty gave a single bark, but Righty had already gone back to sleep.

Bert reached into the paper and pulled out the first chicken leg. He offered it to Lefty, who eagerly gnawed the meat off the end. Bert held the bone still, until Lefty had gotten every last scrap.

He used the bone, cautiously of course, to poke Righty. The second head awoke with a snort, and Bert waved the drumstick under his nose. Righty blinked, and then began devouring the chicken. Bert smiled and held the bone as he had for Lefty. Maybe Righty would start to like him if he kept feeding it.

Bert took a step away, and settled against the wall in a position to see the front of the inn where the adventurers would emerge. He fished out a third chicken leg, and ripped off a mouthful. It was the most heavenly thing he'd ever eaten. Bert scarfed down every scrap of meat, and then spent several minutes licking his hands clean.

Boberton wandered over, and curled up next to Bert. Lefty rested his head on Bert's foot, and the dog's tail thudded on the ground. Then Boberton delivered a thunderous fart, and the paint on the wall behind him began to peel.

"Boberton pungent." Bert waved his hand in front of his nose.

He considered eating the last chicken leg, but figured it would be smart to save some for later. He put the chicken back in his bag, and was about to return to the garbage can when the door to the inn opened, and Master White walked out.

"Time to go, Boberton." He gently shook the dog, who rose quickly, tail wagging furiously.

Crotchshot emerged from the inn a moment later, a tankard clutched in either hand. The dwarf came next, his mouth hanging open and his eyes consumed with the far away look of someone who kind of wished they'd died instead of woken up to find themselves this hung over. Bert sympathized.

Kit came last, the platinum-haired sorceress looking well rested. She cradled her magic staff in one hand, and Bert noted the ruby at the top. "Bet stone worth some gold."

Four hundred gold? Maybe not. Probably not worth stealing, unless she fell asleep and he saw an opportunity.

The adventurers followed White up the street, and to Bert's surprise they simply abandoned their dragon. He picked a wide path around the creature, mostly because of the smell, but also because one never knew when an undead dragon might get hungry.

He hurried after the adventurers, with Boberton ambling proudly next to him. Bert rather liked having a dog, even one who only half liked him. For the first time in, well, ever, he felt like he wasn't alone. "Come on, Boberton. Adventurers will find gold. Normally we take stuff they leave, but this time we steal gold."

Bert had no idea how foolhardy such a plan was, but he was confident that if he found the right opportunity he could take something worth a lot of gold, and then he could buy his warg. He wasn't really sure how it all worked, but theoretically that should give him a full-hit die. He might have as many as eleven points. Then, he'd be feared across the land. The mighty Bert.

They reached a wide cobblestone bridge that arced over a lazy river. Beyond that bridge a sign with a money bag and a present sat in plain view. They must be going to the merchant district.

The bridge had skeletal guards at either end, but those guards didn't bother the adventurers, and they didn't seem to notice either Bert or Boberton. He crept cautiously past them, then sprinted after the party as fast as his stubby legs would allow.

Just beyond the end of the bridge, Bert came skidding to a halt when he realized the adventurers had stopped. They stood outside a three-story brick building with a swaying, wooden sign. That sign had the standard armor and weapon symbols that most shops seemed to favor, but these ones glowed, which Bert guessed meant this was a magic item shop.

He'd always wanted to see a magic item shop.

"Interlopers!" A voice rang out across the morning, echoing down the cobblestones. "Explain yourselves."

Silence fell in its wake. Farmers suddenly found alleyways. Passersby scurried inside shops. Within moments the street was empty, except for the adventurers and whoever had spoken.

Bert stood on his tiptoes, and peered up the hill in the direction the voice had come from. A pale-skinned man that Bert could only classify as beautiful sat astride an enormous, fluffy, white dog. It was literally the best mount that Bert had ever seen. The dog's fur was luxurious, but its fangs were also impressive. Cuddly, but it could fight.

Another man, this one wearing the bright sequins of a bard, stepped in front of the dog. He raised a microphone, and peered over his sunglasses at the adventurers. He had dark skin, and a thin, black beard that hugged his jawline.

"Word in the crypt is that you dusted the great wyrm, Smug. The dark lord sent Edward and I down from the tomb to see if you scrubs know anything about it."

"Ooh." Bert waddled over to the far side of the street, and set down his pack. He patted the ground next to him, and Boberton came over to sit with him. "Adventurers accidentally triggered a boss fight. Going to kill monsters now. Come watch."

9

WHANYE

K it was lost in thought as she approached the magic item shop's oaken door. This was going to be the hardest adventure they'd ever attempted, and she wanted to make sure she picked up the right blend of magic items from the shop.

She had plenty of healing potions, but there were probably some scrolls that would be useful down there, especially if they sold anything third level or higher. More fireballs would be a good thing.

"Interlopers!" A voice like a clarion call split the morning.

She spun to face the road leading up to the tomb, and her heart sank when she spotted the pair of men approaching. She knew both by reputation. Even a basic gather information check had told her all about Baron Kullen, and the bard, Whanye East.

The bard stepped forward, and raised his magical microphone. Kit paid more attention to the man himself than to whatever he was prattling on about. This would come to a fight. She had no doubt about it, and it was her job to make sure her side won.

Sure enough, Crotchshot nocked a trio of arrows, and in the same instant Brakestuff drew his sword and began advancing up the street.

"Oh, boy," she muttered, and raised a hand to start casting a haste spell. "*Inquis Celeritas!*"

A huge symbol appeared on the ground under the party, and burst upwards in a cascade of blue light. The motes clung to each of them, and the magic dramatically increased their speed.

"All right!" Brakestuff screeched, his voice several octaves higher because of the spell. "Let's bring the pain."

"Yo, you're not even gonna answer me about Smug?" The bard seemed deeply offended. He started beatboxing into his microphone, and multicolored magic rippled outward from him, bathing Baron Kullen and the war terrier.

Brakestuff blurred toward the bard, and brought his blade arcing down in a streak of death. Whanye danced out of the way, then came back to his feet and started rapping. "Life's tough on the cobblestone streets, when you gotta deal with deadbeats, fakers, takers, bakers, with muffins, and tuffins, and shit."

Brakestuff lunged forward, and smashed Whanye in the face with his shield. Whanye's nose shattered, splattering the shield with blood. The dwarf grinned up at him. "Bitch, I'm sixth level." His voice was comically high pitched. "That gives me two attacks, but you know what? Haste makes that three."

He swung again, but suddenly Kullen was there. The vampire zipped forward, and caught Brakestuff full in the face with a roundhouse. The kick sent him tumbling across the cobblestones, but the dwarf stubbornly held onto his sword and shield.

"Bah, you hit like a girl." Brakestuff spit onto the ground. "Pretty boy vampire."

"Tortured vampire," Kullen corrected, citing his trope. In that moment, a ray of sun broke the cloud cover, and fell directly on his face. Brilliant light sparkled outward, beautiful and mesmerizing.

Then Crotchshot started firing. Arrow after arrow streaked directly into Kullen's crotch, thudding into a surprisingly small area. Kullen groaned in pain, and clutched at his injured manhood as he collapsed to the ground. "Gnnn. Jacob, kill!"

The terrier surged forward, and leapt on Crotchshot. The archer tried to dodge, but his obvious drunkenness made his leap more of a lurch. The dog knocked him to the cobblestones, and began savaging his throat.

White waved at the nearest group of skeleton guards. "Kill the dog!"

The guards surged forward, clanking across the cobblestones and then ramming their spears into the dog. The terrier yipped, and leapt off of Crotchshot. Its body began to ripple, and a moment later a man stood in the dog's place. He was tall, broad shouldered, and bare chested, wearing nothing but cutoff jeans. Blood came from a wound on his chest, and another on his leg, but they didn't seem to bother him.

"I'll go tell the dark lord!" Then he shifted back into dog form, and bravely ran away.

Crotchshot flipped back to his feet, and nocked an arrow. He took a moment to aim, and then leapt into the air. He fired a single shot at Kullen, who was still clutching his crotch. The arrow punched through his crotch, and continued into Kullen's chest.

"No, not the heart!" Kit yelled. She spun, and dove behind a nearby barrel.

It was too late.

Baron Kullen exploded, and wave after wave of bright, sticky glitter burst all over the street. It covered the walls, the carts, and the horses. Worse, it covered Kit and the rest of her companions. She rose to her feet with a sigh, and wiped glitter from her face. "I hate vampires so much."

"Bad move, suckas." Whanye started dancing to a different beat, which Kit recognized as the preamble to another bard song. "I'm gonna run, run away. Gotta retreat, expeditiously!"

The bard turned and sprinted back up the lane toward the tomb, moving far more swiftly than a horse could run or a dragon could fly.

Kit shook her head sadly. So much for the plan. "Guess the dark lord knows we're coming now."

"Hold my beer." Crotchshot handed Kit a tankard, which she was shocked wasn't empty, and nocked an arrow. Three arrows arced into the air in rapid succession, and they streaked down toward Whanye, just before he reached the safety of the tomb's iron gates.

The arrows slammed into his crotch. Once, twice, and a third time. The bard collapsed with a groan, and didn't rise.

10

PHERMIONE STRANGER

K it was impressed by how quickly Crotchshot and Brakestuff stripped the glitter-covered loot from both Whanye and Baron Kullen, efficiently stacking it into a pile. She knew the drill, and cast a detect magic.

Kullen had been wearing a white shirt, which glowed with abjuration, and had somehow managed to avoid getting any glitter on it. Whanye had been wearing a set of sequined leather armor, which she immediately identified. "The shirt enhances the user's charisma. The leather is +2. Vendor trash—I mean, unless someone likes sequins."

"What about the sunglasses and rings?" White demanded. He hovered over the loot like a falcon about to dive.

She bent to inspect the pile. All three objects were powerful, but the glasses were by far the most powerful. "The sunglasses are glasses of alluring charisma, and give you...wow, a full +6. These things are worth a fortune."

White snatched up the glasses, and immediately put them on. It amplified his douchieness immensely. "These will greatly increase the number of undead I can control. We'll need them for the mission. Perhaps after we finish we can consider selling them, but not before. What about the rings, Kit?"

Her shoulders slumped. "The first one is a ring of protection, +4."

White snatched up the ring, as expected.

"The last one is a ring of luck." Kit reached cautiously for the slender silver band. "Does anyone mind if I take it?"

"Hmm." White eyed the ring with obvious greed.

"You already have two rings," Kit snapped, snatching it up. She slid it around her finger.

White looked surprised, but after a moment gave a shrug and a frown. "Fine, but you'll need to purchase it from the party, with a standard discount, of course."

She didn't bother pointing out that he wasn't paying for any of the items he'd taken. Brake would take White's side, and Crotchshot wouldn't care, so that meant she'd be outvoted...again.

"Of course," she said wearily. "Shall we see about selling the armor and the microphone?"

"Not quite yet." White reached into his robes and produced an annoyingly white trope that hurt her eyes to look at. "I took this from Whanye. What is it?"

"Oh no," she whispered, her eyes widening in horror.

"You recognize it, don't you?" White eyed her suspiciously.

"What is it?" Crotchshot peered down at the trope. "Is it valuable?"

"It's a well actually trope. A powerful one," Kit explained. She hesitated, but they were going to badger this out of her eventually. "It gives a +10 intelligence."

"That's impossible." Brakestuff was finally paying attention. He stomped over to her, and stared at the trope in White's hand. "The highest you can get is a +6."

"From a magical item," Kit corrected. "Tropes can go up to +12. This is one of the most powerful in existence, and definitely the most powerful I've ever seen."

"What's the downside?" Crotchshot asked. "If I used intelligence for my attacks I'd be all over that thing."

Kit folded her arms and took a step back from the trope. "It's a well actually trope. It will require you to correct people, whenever you know they're wrong. It will turn you into a know-it-all. You'll become insufferable."

"But it gives you a +10 int?" White demanded. He extended the trope to her expectantly. "This will make your spells much harder to resist, and give you bonus spells, right?"

"Yes." She reluctantly accepted it. Kit removed her thoughtful pragmatist trope, and shivered as the pale grey teardrop came loose in her hand. She socketed the well actually trope, and winced as she felt the magic flow through her body. There was no immediate change, thankfully. Of course, it might take time for the changes to become clear.

White nodded. "Excellent. More haste spells are a good thing, and perhaps you can pick up some offensive scrolls here so you aren't absolutely worthless. I'll handle the negotiations."

White pushed the door open and headed inside, and Kit waited while Brakestuff and Crotchshot piled in after. She entered after them, her staff thumping across the floor as she peered in wonder at the surrounding walls.

Armor, weaponry, rods, staves...they had it all. The collective magical glow in this place could probably be observed from neighboring kingdoms.

"Shopkeeper," White called in an annoyingly condescending manner. "I have wonderful news. We're going to make you an incredible deal."

"Really?" A bored gnome, not more than two feet tall, adjusted his spectacles behind the counter. He walked across a narrow ledge that had been built behind the counter to accommodate his size. "Bitch, I put everything into social skills. I'm a social god. You think those glasses are going to give you an edge? Check it." He jerked a thumb at a rune-etched headband. "Headband of mental superiority. +6 bonus to all mental stats."

White showed a rare moment of doubt, but it vanished quickly, smothered by his smug superiority. "We're selling an incredibly potent, uh, microphone, and a matching set of armor."

The gnome raised an eyebrow. "Your matching set of armor is leaking blood and glitter on my counter. Did you just kill a vampire outside and take that?"

"Yes," White admitted. He must have rolled terribly on his barter check.

"Tell you what I'm going to do." The gnome hooked both thumbs in his belt. "I'll give you 20% of the market value, and I'll give you a 10% discount on any purchases you make today."

"Fine. You're lucky we're in a hurry." White folded his arms, conceding defeat. "I'm looking for a rod of undead domination. Tell me you have it, and I'll give in to your predatory business practices."

"I want some arrows of lich slaying," Crotchshot broke in. "And a belt of manly strength."

"Well, actually," Kit found herself saying, "you want a greater belt of manly strength. You're already wearing a belt of manly strength." Her hands shot up and she covered her mouth in horror.

She still remembered stories of the first woman to ever possess the well actually trope, Phermione Stranger. She was remembered as one of the most powerful wizards of all time, but she also had no friends, because she needed to be right 100% of the time.

"How about you, little lady?" The gnome asked, peering up at her through his tiny spectacles. "What's your pleasure? Please say gnome."

She sighed, and regretted not taking a male character. "I'll take all of your offensive scrolls between levels three and five. And a disintegrate scroll if you have it."

"Ahh, that last one's sixth level, I'm afraid." The gnome shrugged helplessly. "You'd need a critical success on your barter test, and then maybe I've got it in the back room."

Kit sighed. "White?"

"Master White," the necromancer corrected, glaring at her. "Do you have a disintegrate scroll for sale?"

"Turns out I do." The gnome seemed surprised. "I'll go and fetch it, and I'll grab a mess of fireball scrolls for you. None of the fourth level spells are worth your time, but you might want a couple of the fifth. Cloudkill is no joke."

The gnome walked up his ledge, which disappeared through a curtained doorway into a rear store room. He emerged a moment later with an armload of scrolls.

She began cataloguing them while White reluctantly paid the shopkeeper for everything they'd asked for.

There were six fireball scrolls, which would probably be the most handy. She also had a cloudkill, and something called phantasmal killer.

"So where are you fellas headed, anyway?" the gnome asked.

"We're going to go kill the dark lord," Brakestuff interjected without missing a beat.

Dead silence fell on the rest of the party. Even Crotchshot seemed to realize that the dwarf had said something he shouldn't have.

"Outside, dwarf, now," White thundered. He turned back to the shopkeeper. "It's in your best interest to forget you saw us."

"Yeah, whatever, scrub." The gnome gave a derisive snort. "Any time you wanna dance you come pay me a visit."

Kit stuffed the scrolls into her pack, and followed her party out the door.

11

BLOW THE HORN

Bert huddled in the shadows, watching the adventurers. He badly wanted to steal one of the rings, or maybe the microphone, as that certainly looked valuable enough to trade for a warg. Unfortunately, the adventurers were very focused on their winnings, and Bert wasn't able to gather any of it.

Both he and Boberton were now coated in glitter, which he rather liked. It made him look fancy. Maybe even the fanciest goblin ever. It would probably stick around for a while too, as long as he didn't bathe, which he wouldn't unless he accidentally fell into a pond.

Bert waited patiently, and it didn't take long for the adventurers to emerge from the magic item shop. He'd considered following them inside, but had no idea if there might be spells that could kill a goblin. He'd rather not find out.

White started up the narrow lane that snaked toward the tomb. The necromancer sported a new snowy-white cloak, and held a long, black rod with a menacing skull in his right hand. The rest of his party followed, and Bert waddled after them as fast as he could. He looked forward to letting Boberton, or maybe a warg someday, do the waddling.

As the squat, foreboding tomb loomed larger on the hill, Bert had a lot of time to think. How were the adventurers going to get inside? Maybe he could try to get their attention, and offer to give them the moat slug's intel. Of course, he still needed to get that intel, which is why he waited. He had a drumstick in his backpack, and he bet he could trade it to the slug. If only he had time.

The adventurers continued boldly up the cobblestones, and the higher they climbed, the fewer people they passed. A chill wind picked up, and Bert saw more and more ravens perched in the dead trees lining the path. Thunder rolled in the distance.

Boberton gave a pitiful whine, and Bert patted him reassuringly. "Is okay, Boberton. Adventurers kill everything. Just stay back with Bert, and be very quiet. Can you be quiet, boy?"

Boberton stopped whining, and moved to stand behind Bert. "Good dog."

Bert hurried after the adventurers, and things got creepier with every step. Ghostly grey spirits drifted in and out of sight, always on the edge of vision. If you turned to face one directly, it dissipated and appeared somewhere else.

"Damn it!" Brakestuff snapped. He swung his sword at one of the shades, but it dissolved long before his blade reached it. "I wish these things weren't just part of the scenery. I can't even target them."

"We'll be past them soon enough," White replied, in a placating way that still managed to be condescending. Bert was glad he never needed to talk to White. He didn't like the necromancer very much.

Lightning split the sky above them, and Boberton suddenly knocked Bert to the stone as the dog tried to hide both his faces in Bert's chest. Bert patted the dog again. "It's okay. Just spooky weather. Part of ambience. Won't hurt us."

The sky darkened, and by the time they reached the tall, oaken doors leading into the tomb, Bert had to squint to avoid tripping over the cracks in the cobblestones.

The adventurers had stopped outside, and each had drawn their weapons. Bert slunk a little closer, then stood behind a dead shrub while he listened to their plan. If they got stuck maybe he could be useful. That seemed unlikely though. Usually their plan involved kicking the front door in and murdering everything in the dungeon. Sneaky side entrances didn't seem like their thing.

"How do we want to play this?" Kit asked. The sorceress sounded weary.

"Blow the horn?" Brakestuff suggested. He reached into his pack and pulled out a large ram's horn. Bert still wasn't sure if it was magical, or if the dwarf simply enjoying blowing the horn.

"Why mess with what works?" Crotchshot said. He nocked three arrows. "Kick in the door, blow the horn, and clear the first floor in one go. We can camp to get our spells back, and sweep our way down a level at a time."

Kit planted her hands on her hips, and rolled her eyes at Crotchshot. "What if we blow the horn and a bunch of monsters we can't handle show up? We don't know what's in there, and it won't take—"

Brakestuff lived up to his name, and Bert winced as the dwarf's boot impacted against the door. The gigantic door was blown off its hinges, and clattered inside the hall with a tremendous boom.

"I'm sure they must have heard that," Kit said. The

sorceress took a step closer to the dwarf. "Surely we don't need to—"

The dwarf raised the horn to his lips and blew. A tremendous *DooooDOOOOOOOOOO* echoed through the manor, and down into the city.

"It doesn't hurt to be thorough," Crotchshot pointed out as he advanced through the door, nocked arrow sweeping the room. "Good job, Brake."

"Thanks." The dwarf clapped his sword against his shield, and then gave a joyous whoop. "Oh, man, I can't wait to drop some undead. I can channel holy energy seven times a day now, and it does 5d6 damage to all undead within thirty feet. Plus, it heals you guys."

"Do not channel unless I order it," White snapped. He stepped through the gap where the door used to be, and moved into the darkness. Shadows covered the top half of his face when he turned back to them, making his eyes glitter in the darkness. "I can dominate many of these undead. Don't slay them unless I am unable to subdue them. Each one we add to our number can be used to slay the dark lord in the bowels of this place."

Clanking footsteps sounded in the distance, and Bert briefly considered how to handle this. In the past he'd always hung back while the adventurers fought. He wasn't likely to draw their attention, but a stray attack might kill him if he wasn't careful.

But if he waited out here he was never going to get enough money to buy a warg. He needed to get to the loot, some of it at least, before the adventurers. Bert turned to Boberton. "Bert going inside. Very dangerous. Boberton stay here, okay?"

Boberton gave a deep whine and paced back and forth. "Dog not going to wait here?"

Boberton blinked at him.

"Okay, dog can come." Bert held a finger up to his lips. "Be quiet, and stay close. No barking!"

Boberton's jaw clicked shut, and his tail drooped. Bert took that as agreement. He turned back to the manor, and slipped inside.

The adventurers had moved to the middle of a wide marble mausoleum, and stood in a loose arrangement, ready to attack anything that emerged from the pair of shadowed hallways disappearing into the distance.

Bert looked around the room. There were a few statues, but they were too large. He needed something Bert-sized. He hugged the wall, and crept his way along it until he reached one of the statues. He huddled behind the base, and pulled Boberton into hiding as well. He'd explore a bit once the adventurers dealt with the monsters.

This was a dangerous game, but Bert was a dangerous goblin.

12
———

SIR PATRICK

Kit cocked her head and judged the footsteps echoing up the corridor that fed into the tomb's entry hall. She waited until the last possible instant, and then cast her haste spell. The familiar symbol flashed up, bathing the party in its potent magical energy. The power thrummed through her, accelerating her mind, her body, and her voice, unfortunately.

Brakestuff moved protectively to the front of the party, and raised his tower shield high as the first enemies flowed up the corridor. The dwarf turned back to face them, his voice chipmunk-high. "Looks like we got shadows. Watch those drain attacks."

Kit reached into her pack and withdrew the first fireball scroll. She cracked the seal, and studied the magical symbols on the page. The moment she saw the first pair of hellish, red eyes she began to cast. "*De facto Ignis Sphera et cetera!*"

The words burned away from the page, and the paper burst into a ball of dense, blue flame. It streaked toward the shadows, and detonated in their midst.

A forty-foot wave of crackling flame rushed outwards, engulfing the shadows, and drawing shrieks from the evil creatures. Two melted into smoky wisps that quickly dissipated, but the rest glared hatefully as they surged forward.

"Not on my watch, scum." Brakestuff sprinted into the shadows, and raised his hands as he channeled his god's holy might. "Knowsbest, grant me your strength!"

A wave of pure, golden light, as true as the sun, but easier to look upon, blazed toward the shadows. A rapid chorus of shrieks began, and then ceased as the creatures dissolved into nothingness.

"But I didn't even get to shoot anything," Crotchshot groused. He gave an exaggerated sigh. "I hate rolling low on initiative. That shouldn't even be possible with my bonuses."

Low, feral growls came from the hallway as pallid, chitinous humanoids advanced in a mass. Their gnashing, inhuman teeth glittered cruelly in the torchlight.

"More fireballs," White snapped. He gesticulated with his staff. "End them!"

Kit gritted her teeth. "But you said that we shouldn't attack until—"

"These are just ghouls," White overrode her. "Kill them."

Kit read another scroll, and as before, blue flame streaked into her enemies. This time, though, the spell's detonation had considerably less effect, other than pushing a wave of cooked putrescence in their direction. "Well, that was super effective."

A few of the ghouls hung back, wisps of smoke rising from their skin. Most hadn't even suffered that much, though, and were advancing en masse toward Brakestuff.

The dwarf raised his stubby arms again, and another wave of holy energy rippled outwards. The ghouls cringed, and one gave a shriek as its body burst into purifying flame. But the rest kept coming.

They rushed forward in a frantic mass, rolling over Brake in a tide of pasty-white bodies. The dwarf went down underneath the mob, shouting as he struggled to get back to his feet.

"Keep fireballing!" White ordered. "Crotchshot, get to work."

"Can't you control them?" Crotchshot complained. "It will take like six arrows to kill each one."

"I'm saving my spells for the true threats. This is the preamble, my friend."

"Okay." Crotchshot raised his bow and took aim at the most wounded ghoul. Three arrows streaked into its crotch, and the creature doubled over with a groan. "Oh, must have gotten a crit. Nice."

Kit considered another fireball, as White had ordered, but there was too large a chance it would hit Brakestuff. He had a lot of hit points, but she didn't like the idea of scorching a friend.

Clattering footsteps came from the distance, and a half dozen zombie archers, undead versions of Crotchshot, stepped into view. They loosed a volley of arrows at the elf, and Crotchshot dodged as best he could. He avoided some, but an arrow thudded into his shoulder, and another sank into his knee.

"Ahhhh! Arrow to the knee," he screamed, dropping prone and cradling his injured leg with both hands. "My career is over. I'll have to take a job as some shitty guard in a random town."

Kit felt more than heard heavy footsteps approaching behind the archers. Malevolent eyes shone in the darkness, higher up than the shadows had been. Whatever this was, it was much taller, and much more powerful. The menacing figure took several clanking steps forward, into the light.

"Oh, shit," Kit whispered. "That's a death knight." She began casting her best defensive spell. "*Status quo verbatim specula imago!*"

Four exact duplicates sprung out of Kit, appearing all around her. The images shifted and moved, making it impossible to tell which was real. That wouldn't keep her alive for long, but it bought her time, and often served as enough deterrent that people attacked Brake instead.

The knight raised a thick, black sword easily in one hand, and pointed at them. His cultured voice echoed up the corridor as he stepped into the great hall. "Adventurers come into our city, and we fall back. They kill our sparkly vampires, and we fall back. You have the temerity to kick in our front door? To blow a bloody hunting horn? No more. Not again. The line must be drawn *here*." He scratched a line of sparks along the dank stone. "This far, and no farther. My name is Sir Patrick, once the staunchest captain to ever know war. And I will make you pay for what you've done."

A wave of black light pulsed outward from the death knight, crashing over all of them. Kit's mind filled with mind-blanking terror, and her only thought was that she must get away.

Crotchshot was wounded. Brakestuff struggled under a pile of ghouls, and his struggles seemed to be growing weaker. The death knight's fear aura wasn't the only thing making her want to run.

White lunged out of the shadows suddenly, and aimed the black rod with the gothic skull at the knight. "*Verbatim quod dictis!*"

A ray of scarlet shot into the death knight's face, and the magic rippled over him, its tendrils binding him into place, but only for a moment. They seeped into the black armor, and the eyes flared scarlet before returning to their eerie green.

White folded his arms and leaned back smugly. "Now, order your minions to cease attacking."

The knight's hellish, inhuman gaze studied the necromancer. He was silent for several moments.

"Do as he says." The knight waved at the ghouls, who reluctantly stopped munching on Brakestuff.

The ghouls allowed the dwarf to climb to his feet, though he'd lost both his sword and shield. He didn't seem to have suffered any real damage.

"And drop the fear aura," White commanded.

"Fine." The knight waved in her direction, and the terror abruptly ceased.

Kit sucked in a deep breath as full control returned to her body. Crotchshot, who'd been crawling away as fast as he could manage, stopped, and pulled his back against a pillar. "My knee..."

"Now, approach, knight." White crooked a finger, and began tapping his foot.

"As you wish." The death knight gave a heavy sigh, and clanked his way over.

"Don't be too embarrassed." White waved the rod of undead domination triumphantly. "You really stood no chance."

The death knight's armor creaked as he shrugged. "It is possible to commit no mistakes and still lose. That is not weakness. I feel no shame. Nor do I have any love for the master of this place. He is utterly mad, as you'll soon find."

Just like that, they'd gone from life and death to having their own small army. Despite White being, well, himself, she was genuinely impressed. But she also felt like she could sleep for a week, and they were still on the first level.

13

BAD DOG

Kit moved to stand next to White, and watched silently as he interrogated the death knight. Behind her she could hear the *bawhump* that came each time Brake used one of his channels to heal himself or Crotchshot. She tuned them out, and focused on the death knight.

"What's your name?" White demanded.

"I already gave it. I am called Sir Patrick." The knight planted the tip of his enormous sword against the stone, and pointedly leaned on it. His eyes narrowed and surged with white flames. "And how shall I address you, master?"

"Call me...Lord White," the necromancer proclaimed. A grin appeared on his smarmy features. "Yes, I like the sound of that."

"I don't," Kit supplied without thinking. White eyed her sharply, but she stood her ground and rolled her eyes. "Oh, come on. You don't expect me to call you Lord White, do you? What are you the lord of? You're lucky we give you the master title."

White's eyes flashed, and momentary rage flitted across his face. "You *will* learn to respect me, sorceress. I can promise you that."

Kit was horrified by her own behavior. The well actually trope was already getting her into trouble. White could hold a grudge, and increasingly he was the group's leader. If she alienated him she could find herself on the wrong side of a cell, or worse, forced to find a new adventuring group to hang out with. That meant making real friends, in the real world.

"I'm sorry, Master White." Kit delivered the apology with sincerity, and gave him a bow from the waist to show she meant it. His features relaxed, and she breathed an internal sigh of relief. She turned to the strange knight. "Sir Patrick, can you tell us what to expect between here and the dark lord?"

"Do not order my minions about." Master White glared at her, looking every inch the pompous title. Then he turned to the knight. "Sir Patrick, what awaits us on the levels below? Should we rest before proceeding?"

Sir Patrick's aged face grew somber. "It will not be easy. The next level belongs to a powerful mummy, the dark lord's most trusted servant." The knight shook his head as he surveyed the party. "My minions cannot help you, and you are not up to the task. I believe most of you will die. All of you if you attempt anything other than sneaking through Ramen Brotep's domain."

"Tell me of this fearsome mummy." White wore his hunger openly. "He must have a weakness."

Sir Patrick laughed. "None that I know of."

Kit folded her arms, and risked speaking to the knight. "And what makes him so dangerous? Is he a sorcerer?"

"Of a sort. He practices the forbidden art of adoramancy, and is rumored to be a nekomancer." Patrick's features expressed the very last expression she'd expected. Fear. "I'd advise you not to underestimate him. His lair is littered with statues, every one a would-be hero trying to reach the dark lord."

"He uses petrification then?" Kit asked.

Sir Patrick nodded. He lifted the tip of his blade from the stone. "I am immune to such magics, but I can do nothing to shield you, Lord White. I would advise you to martial your strength, and strike when you are rested. Brotep will not leave his lair, and we are likely safe until we descend. I will keep watch, if you wish."

"Yes, do that." White waved dismissively, then walked to the corner the room where he began inspecting his new minions.

Kit's shoulders slumped. She was even more exhausted now. The others were already making camp, and would expect her to make dinner soon. She didn't feel like dealing with it. Kit retreated to her own corner, and willed herself into fox form.

Her body rippled and shifted, her point of view dropping, while her body became smaller and furrier. Fox form was a much better way to rest, not just because it was warmer, but also because it was safer. Most people would leave her alone, assuming she was a regular fox, or at worst a familiar.

She turned in a slow circle, and then settled down atop her pack as she prepared for sleep. Kit was just beginning to nod off when a sudden, and very urgent, barking began. She opened her eyes to find a demo pup barking fiercely up at her.

The small red dog had two heads, both equally incensed

by her existence. It was the very last creature she'd have expected to encounter in the midst of a dungeon of this magnitude. Kit rose and stretched, and then hopped down off her pack to sniff the pup.

It wore a collar, which was attached to a leash, and that leash...wait, was it being held by a critter? She blinked down at a terrified goblin who was desperately tugging on the pup's collar to pull it away from her. "No! Bad dog. Shhhhh. Boberton get Bert into trouble."

Kit shifted back to elven form, and dropped down into a squat next to the goblin. He wasn't quite tall enough to reach her knee, and he was covered in glitter. He must have been outside the tomb when Baron Kullen exploded. "Your name is Bert? What are you doing here? This is an undead dungeon. You shouldn't be anywhere near here. Did you get lost somehow?"

"Uh." The goblin blinked up at her, and his mouth worked as if trying to find better words. "Bert sorry. Bert will go away."

"Wait." She moved a hand down to block his exit. The dog leaned over and sniffed it. One of the heads gave her an experimental lick, though the other one had closed its eyes and was now snoring softly. "How did you get in here?"

"Uhhh..." The goblin looked around her hand and seemed to realize he couldn't escape. He promptly sat down, and looked up at her with those big eyes. "Bert tell truth, and suffer consequences. Bert follow you for long time." He counted all his fingers on both hands, then repeated it. "Four hands, and three fingers of days."

"Why?" She folded her arms, both curious and a little scandalized that this critter had apparently managed to shadow them for weeks. Had this been what she'd felt when they fought the dragon?

"Bert want gold," he explained enthusiastically. He set his pack down next to him, and reached inside, then extended a large, brown pellet to the dog. The dog scarfed it down. "Bert need 400 pieces of gold, then Bert can buy warg. Go back to Paradise and be warg rider."

She glanced down at his chest and noted that his trope socket was empty. Of course it was. Critters didn't have tropes. Her eyes widened as her newly enhanced intellect effortlessly connected the dots. "You think that if you get this warg it will turn you into a warg rider?"

He nodded eagerly, and a wide grin split his sparkly, pale green face.

Kit didn't have the heart to tell him the truth. Especially not after the ingenuity he'd shown in following them. "So how do you make your money?"

"Uh." He scuffed the dirt with a foot and avoided looking at her. "Bert take copper, and sometimes silver, that adventurers leave behind."

Kit burst out laughing. It felt good, genuine, and easy. "You're a scavenger, then. It seems to be working well for you. Who's your friend?" She petted the pup, whose tail thumped against her leg.

"Boberton." Bert straightened, and adopted a dignified air. "Bert have to take care of Boberton. Bought him from the monster shop."

A critter with a pet. She thought she'd seen it all, but this was simultaneously the sweetest and funniest thing she'd seen in a while. "I'm okay with you following us, but you have to be very careful, and make sure you stay way behind us. Only come down when the fighting stops, okay?"

Bert nodded cautiously, but she wasn't sure he was taking it seriously. "I really mean it. Don't follow us until you know it's safe."

He nodded again. "Can Bert go now? Promise Boberton won't bother you. Will stop his barking."

She hid her smile behind her hand. "Of course, Bert. It was nice to meet you."

Kit shifted back into fox form, and settled down to sleep, her heart lighter than it had been.

14

BEST FRIEND

Bert waddled away feeling a bit taller than when he'd approached his new friend. He turned to Boberton, who was trotting alongside him now, and no longer wanted to bark. "Bert likes pretty elf lady. She talk to Bert like Bert adventurer. Bert proud."

Boberton's tongue lolled out of Lefty's mouth, and he seemed to pick up on Bert's mood. Bert brought him all the way to the far corner of the room, behind a pillar. There was a small area shrouded in complete darkness, and there was no reason for an adventurer to come back here since there was nothing to be looted.

Bert set up Boberton's bedroll, and made sure the pup was comfortable. Once Boberton was nice and cozy, Bert left him and started to explore. There could be all sorts of loot in this room, and if not it would tucker him out so he could get some sleep.

He prowled the entry way, focusing particularly on darkened areas around pillars, since any shiny objects discarded there wouldn't reflect light, thus making them harder to find. They were more likely to be overlooked.

One by one the adventurers laid down to sleep, though the white necromancer stayed up after the others. Bert didn't like the way he looked at Kit, or at any of the others. He studied them as they slept, and then finally went to sleep.

Bert ignored the creepy necromancer, and focused on getting rich. After another hour or so of searching he found a rock in the shadow of a pillar. As he'd done with the other rocks, Bert held it up to the light. This time the rock glinted.

He hurried over to the light of the adventurers' campfire and held the rock up. Bert gasped. It was a red stone, and it was pretty. He didn't know what kind of gemstone it might be, but it was probably worth a lot of gold. Four hundred gold? Maybe.

Should he leave and go sell it? If it was worth enough he wouldn't have to risk descending through the rest of the tomb, which he didn't mind admitting terrified him.

"No," he said, balling his little hands into fists. "Staying dangerous, but Bert brave. If Bert leaves now, and gem isn't worth enough gold, then Bert will have to come back. Bert will stay."

He looked over at Kit, the small, furry version of her. The fox was asleep against Kit's pack, a magical staff propped against the wall behind him.

It wasn't likely Bert would be able to help Kit, but this place was dangerous, and maybe he could do something if he followed her. Plus, he needed to find more loot. Better loot. That meant getting there first.

He wondered what the adventurers were after here. Something worth a lot more than four hundred gold, probably. Like five hundred.

Bert headed back over to his little camp where Boberton's heads were snoring in a synchronized harmony. Bert reached into his pack and got out his backup blanket, and settled it over Boberton. Then he pulled his bedroll over to the dog, and lay down next to his best friend.

He could say that now, because he had two friends, if he counted Kit. Bert smiled, and drifted off to sleep.

15

RAMEN BROTEP

K it woke up in the quiet predawn hour to find everyone asleep, except for White. He sat studying a spell book, and judging from the leathery pages and dark red script she was fairly certain she didn't want to know what it had been bound from.

Lawful good, her ass. She wished alignment counted for something beyond a label on your character sheet.

She quietly shifted back to elven form, and quickly performed a prestidigitation spell to clean off the previous day's grime. The spell was amazing, and allowed her to clean both herself and her clothing, instantly. It was the primary reason she'd wanted to learn magic when she was a child, because she'd hated carrying laundry down to the river.

Wait, that wasn't her childhood, was it? Not the real her. That was her character. The game was so good at pulling her in, and making her forget that anything else existed.

"Let's get them up." White's voice rang out in the cavernous entry hall. He deposited his book into his pack, then turned to the bedrolls near the fire they'd erected.

White roused the rest of the party, and they quickly broke down camp. It was something they did often, and did in relative silence. Kit put on her pack, and moved to stand behind Brakestuff. Smart casters followed the tank, and while the dwarf could be insufferable at times, he was very good at keeping the rest of them alive.

Brakestuff had already donned his pack, but stood leaning on his tower shield while he waited for Crotchshot, always the last to be ready.

"Almost done," the elf mumbled as he finished brushing his teeth. He spit, then wiped the brush and put it back in his bag. "I don't want to get mouth rot."

"We have a paladin with cure disease," White pointed out. He raised an eyebrow. "Our time is valuable."

"Yeah, well, so's mine." Crotchshot shrugged his pack on. "I don't work for you, necro."

"What did you call me?" White's words were soft, but his gaze was hard. He walked to stand before the elf. "Go on, say it again."

"Uh, never mind." Crotchshot said, backing away. "It ain't worth it. Just don't be thinking you can go around giving me orders. We're all equal here."

"No, we're not." White corrected. He turned to Brakestuff. "As a paladin of Knowsbest, your judgement is impeccable. What's Crotchshot's alignment?"

"Chaotic neutral," the dwarf supplied. He hefted his shield. "And therefore heretical. He's only out for himself. It isn't as bad as a true evil character, mind you, but it's only one step removed."

"And the sorceress?" He didn't even look in her direction, and Kit didn't bother hiding her annoyance.

"True neutral. She's unpredictable, and therefore her judgement can't be trusted." The dwarf stroked his beard with his free hand. "Course, she's also a great support caster, and she's always done right by me. So I say she's okay, even if her judgement is questionable."

"And my own?" White asked, his smile growing more smug by the moment.

"Lawful good, of course." The dwarf gave White a respectful nod. "Your judgement is impeccable. Just like mine."

White turned back to Crotchshot, and smiled cruelly. "So you see, my bow-toting friend, I *am* the leader. I have the tank's support, and the tank is also the healer. We're here to do good, not line your pockets. Try to remember that."

Crotchshot mumbled something that sounded like an apology, but he glared at White, behind his back at least. Kit actually felt a little sorry for the ranger, and was mildly grateful she hadn't been the subject of White's attention. His aura of insufferable-ness was mounting, and quickly. As long as he had Brakestuff's support there was really no stopping him.

"Now then." White picked up his pack and started for the corridor that descended into the darkness. "Shall we deal with this Ramen Brotep? Sir Patrick, you say you cannot help us?"

"My powers are worthless in Brotep's domain." The knight shook his head sadly. "I can pass through, but I cannot do anything. I'll be there watching, of course, but beyond answering any questions you might have, my aid is limited."

"Very well." White gave a disappointed sigh. "I suppose it will have to do. Brake, take point. Let's see if we can find out why this 'adoramancer' is so feared."

The dwarf started up the corridor, and White trailed

after. Crotchshot gave a very quiet sigh, then joined them. Kit considered for a moment, then shifted back into fox form. It meant leaving her pack here, but beyond the risk of Bert rummaging through it, there was no real danger in leaving it here.

She sensed that being in fox form might save her life in the very near future. She had no idea what this mummy could do, but the idea of being petrified scared her more than most potential deaths. Could those people still sense their surroundings? Or dream? Were they dead? She did not want to find out.

Kit crept after the rest of the party, which slowed as they approached torchlight at the base of the corridor. It spilled into a wide, sand-covered room. Obelisks towered into the shadows near the top of the cavern, only the hieroglyph-covered bases visible from their vantage up the corridor.

Scattered throughout the room were dozens of statues, each frozen into a similar position. Most were squatting down, and instead of horror their faces reflected...bliss? It was the kind of expression you wore when you saw something really cute, which fit the adoramancer title.

"I will see you on the far side," Sir Patrick said. He walked calmly through the room.

As he crossed the sand, a faint whispering began. It came from everywhere at once, many voices overlapping. Kit tensed, ready to bolt if it came to it.

Something small and white scampered into view. Then another. And another. Dozens of the creatures swarmed across the sand.

"Awwwww," Crotchshot crooned. "They're kittens. Look how cute they are."

They were kittens, not more than two weeks old. Most were still in that awkward stage where they couldn't quite make their bodies do what they wanted. Every last kitten wore a pharaonic headdress, the bright gold cloth extra cute against their fluffy fur.

"You may go pet them, if you wish." White waved at the cats.

White never did anything that magnanimous, and she puzzled out his motive quickly enough. White wanted to see what would happen, and was using the elf as bait.

Crotchshot walked cautiously into the room, an arrow nocked as he took a few steps into the room. Nothing happened. He moved to the first croup of kittens, and eased his arrow on the bowstring so he could reach down and pet the closest one.

"It's been a long time," came a raspy voice from the shadows at the far end of the room. "Not too many make it past Sir Patrick. He's a hardcore motherfucker."

"You're damned right," Sir Patrick confirmed as he reached an obelisk near where the voice had originated. "I got cheezed. It doesn't count."

A mummy stepped into view, his body wrapped in thick strips of cloth, which had been fused to his body during the mummification. His eyes were bordered by bright red skin, probably a result of the natron salt used to preserve him.

The mummy gave Sir Patrick a high five, and then a bro fist, and then a hug. "After I turn this fool to stone you'll be back to your old self. Yo, you got plans later?"

Crotchshot had just started to pet a small, white siamese when a wave of magic pulsed from Brotep. It wasn't a spell, as there was no visible casting, so it must be a spell-like ability. Those had slightly different rules, and were much more rare.

The magic seeped into every kitten in the room, and they all gave a collective, "MEW!"

The sound reverberated through the room, but Crotchshot didn't seem to notice. He merely sat there, petting the kitten as flaky, grey stone began to grow on his arms, and then his legs, and then his head. Within moments his entire body had turned to granite, his hand still extended to pet the siamese.

Kit looked down at the sand. Should she risk sprinting through the room? She might make it. Or she might die. She looked over her shoulder at the stairs, and considered running. She loved kittens as much as the next adventurer, but she wasn't in a hurry to spend her life as a statue.

16

GOOD DOG

Bert second guessed himself multiple times as he followed Kit down the gently sloping corridor. Every step took more courage as he waddled down to the next level, but it helped to have Boberton plodding along right beside him. Every time Bert woke up the dog was a little larger, and it was getting harder and harder to control him with the leash.

Thankfully, Boberton was usually well behaved, though it worried Bert that if Boberton got too unruly he wouldn't be able to stop the dog. He made a mental note to have a serious talk with Boberton as soon as they were somewhere safe, so he could explain how dangerous being a dog could be.

Torchlight flickered in the distance, and they finally reached a wide opening that looked out on a sand-covered room. Large, spiky stones with weird writing on them dotted the room, but what caught Bert's attention was the statues. There were a lot of them, and every one had once been an adventurer.

And then the trouble began.

Bert recognized the sound at once, and began to shiver with fright. Dealing with dragons and death knights was one thing, but...cats? There was nothing more terrifying than cats. Paradise was, by and large, a safe place. Their only danger, and the reason they needed warg riders in the first place was the cats who ruled the dump.

The sounds Bert was hearing came from young cats, at least. That meant they'd be slow, but they still had sharp claws and Bert would need to take great care. He clung tightly to Boberton's leash, and crept to the edge of the room.

The elf had already gone inside, and for some insane reason he was putting the hand within clawing distance of a small, white cat. As expected, the baby cat viciously pounced on the hand, but the elf seemed amused, instead of hurt.

More cats crawled across the sand, a tide of awkward cat-lings intent on devouring the elf's flesh. Bert was certain of it. That's the only thing cats were good for. He wanted to warn the elf, but knew that Crotchshot couldn't see him, and wouldn't listen even if he could.

He watched with empathetic horror as every cat in the room began to mew at the same time. The magic rippled over the elf, and his skin began to turn to stone. Bert's shoulders slumped. Within a few seconds Crotchshot was no different than any other statue in the room.

One of the most powerful adventurers in the world had been overcome by cat-lings. Bert studied the others to see how they'd react, and wasn't surprised to find terrified expressions. Even White looked paler than usual, and he was made from arrogance and derision, too proud to feel fear.

Bert pulled Boberton closer to him as he watched Kit trot across the sand in the room. Her fear was so strong that he could smell it, and he wished he had a way to protect her. She and the others began making their way across the sand.

On the far side, Bert realized, stood a strange-looking monster Bert had never seen before. He was wrapped in thick bandages, the kind you put over bad cuts, and also wore several gold chains with big amulets on them. It was very gaudy, but the mummy—that's what they'd called it—seemed quite proud of them.

"That man controlling cats," Bert realized aloud. "Bert stop. Kit be safe." But how could he stop him? Bert looked around and realized that the brackets holding the torches were low enough that he could clamber up and get on. He hurried over to the closest torch, and awkwardly scrambled up the stones until he could reach the torch.

Bert used one slender hand to bat at the torch, until it clattered to the ground in a shower of sparks. Bert dropped back down, and heaved it into the air with both hands. He turned to Boberton, straining under the weight. "Boberton, scare cats. Bark at them. Make cats run away!"

Boberton seemed to understand, and immediately charged at the closest group of cats, the ones near Kit. They took one look at the demo pup, and their tails poofed out like pine trees. They began running away, but Boberton chased after them. He barked at many kittens, and they all started running.

Bert used the opportunity to slowly cross the room. The torch was heavy, so he took his time crossing the sand. The mummy didn't seem to see him, and was focused solely on the adventurers. "Nah, nah, nah. It's not going down like that. I don't know how y'all managed to scare the cats in my anti-magic field, but I just gotta calm them down, and then you suckers are toast."

The mummy held up a wand, and aimed it at the cats. He began chanting in a language Bert didn't know, the same one Kit used, he was fairly sure.

Bert hummed to himself as he carefully maneuvered behind the mummy, then dipped the torch down and touched it to the mummy's right leg. The wrappings went up as if doused in oil, but Bert touched the torch to the other leg, and the butt, just to be certain.

Flames began licking up the mummy's body, and the mummy began shrieking and beating at his legs. "Holy crap, I'm on fire! This ain't worth it. I'm out." The mummy rolled toward the sand, and sank down into it as if the sand were several feet deep or more. The flames were extinguished as the mummy disappeared, leaving nothing but a wisp of oily smoke in his wake.

Bert smiled proudly, and ran over to collect Boberton. The dog was still chasing kittens around, barking. "Good dog. Come with Bert. Time to go."

Boberton turned to face him, and his tail began to wag. The dog trotted dutifully after him as Bert hurried across the sand and out the other side of the room. The sand ended at the edge of the room, giving way to wet stones that sloped down into the darkness.

Bert didn't want to go by himself. He turned back to the room with the mummy, and was relieved to see Kit sprint into the tunnel, her bushy, red tail held high above her. Brakestuff came panting into the corridor a moment later, quickly followed by Master White.

Bert had just saved their lives with the mummy, hadn't he? Wait, Bert had really done that. He hugged Boberton, which the dog seemed to very much like. Lefty began licking his face. "Boberton and Bert did it. Lit mummy on fire. Foof. Scared kitties, no more statues."

Bert proudly sat down and fished out the last drumstick. He ripped off a piece of meat for himself, and gave the rest to Boberton.

Maybe he was getting the hang of this adventurer stuff.

17

FIBONOK SEQUENCE

Kit's heart thundered in her vulpine chest as she sprinted through the sandy room, dodging around kittens. Fear blanked out conscious thought, and her only objective was reaching the yawning stone doorway leading to the next level.

The mummy, Brotep, stood near it, laughing as the kittens swarmed toward Brakestuff and White. A few were after her as well, but they were much slower than she was, and she nimbly vaulted them, while avoiding eye contact.

Sharp yapping came from behind her and she darted a look back to see Boberton chasing several kittens. They scattered before the demo pup, each head losing its shit like the mailman was coming to murder the entire family.

The little dog created a surprising amount of chaos, and managed to keep the kittens away from Brake as the dwarf trotted across the room, his plate armor slowing him.

Kit shifted back to running, and wondered how she was going to get past the mummy. His magic was likely powerful, and she didn't know which of her spells might take him out. Cloudkill wouldn't work, as he didn't need to breathe.

Fireball might have some effect, but it would also hit her friends.

Maybe she could dodge past him? She sprinted low and fast along the ground, her four legs giving her greater speed and control than she'd ever have as an elf.

The mummy shifted in her direction, those awful, dead eyes fixing on her. A bandaged hand rose to cast some sort of spell, something high level that Kit knew she wouldn't survive. Then the mummy's right leg burst into flame.

Brotep peered around trying to find the source, but the mummy's left leg, and his ass, also burst into flames. The mummy spun in a circle, but couldn't seem to locate his attacker. Kit smiled, and kept running. She knew who it had to have been. She ran low across the sand, and sprinted through the stone doorway and onto the next level.

A moment later Boberton came trotting through, but she didn't see Bert. She looked around carefully, but even a full perception check didn't reveal him. Where was he?

White came tumbling out, quickly followed by Brakestuff.

The dwarf planted his hands against the wall, and panted heavily as he struggled to catch his breath. Once it had calmed a little he looked up at White. "I don't know what you did, Master White, but I'm grateful. How did you deal with the mummy? He just dove right into the sand, and the cats started running around like they was gettin' chased."

White's pallor faded as he seemed to recognize he was no longer in danger. He adjusted his hair, then faced the dwarf. "I used a powerful banishment spell to scare the mummy away. He'll be back, but by that time we'll be long gone. Shall we proceed?"

"A powerful banishment spell?" Kit protested. She

stabbed an accusing finger in his direction. "You didn't cast anything the entire time we were in there. You had nothing to do with our survival."

"Oh, really?" The dwarf raised a bushy, scarlet eyebrow as he released the wall. His breathing had largely returned to normal. "Then how did we survive, missy? All I saw was you running like a little bitch."

"Like a little vixen," she corrected automatically. "We survived because..." She trailed off. If she told them about Bert there was a chance they'd kill him. Bert was a goblin, and all goblins were considered evil, though being a critter meant that Bert didn't have an alignment. No, she couldn't put him in danger. "Well, I don't know how, but I didn't see White do anything. Did you?"

"Well, no," he admitted. The dwarf frowned at White. "I trust him, though. He's lawful good. What reason would he have to lie? If he were lying, the only benefit would be stealing credit for an idea that wasn't his, but Master White doesn't need to do that. We all know he's the brains here."

"Really?" Kit snapped. "He's the brains? You made me take a well actually trope, which amped my intelligence up to a superhuman 26. That's 8 points higher than my racial maximum, and 12 points higher than White."

"Bah, you know what I mean." Brakestuff waved dismissively at her, and started up the corridor. "He's the leader. He's got the plans and the ideas. You just know stuff. Plus, you're kind of a heathen. I mean, true neutral? Who picks that alignment?"

"Druids, and people who like balance," she protested, almost in spite of herself. She knew this argument was a lost cause, but she couldn't make herself stop.

"Balance?" The dwarf gave a snort. "You mean we should always let some evil people exist? I rest my case. Your judgement can't be trusted. Stop trying to sabotage White. I know you're jealous."

"Jealous?" she choked out.

Kit finally lapsed into silence, and fell a few steps back as White and Brakestuff advanced up the corridor. A torch hung along the wall every fifty feet or so, making long shadows in between. Kit darted glances behind her, and tension left her shoulder blades when she saw Bert's tiny legs pumping to keep up with Boberton.

She glanced at her party, but neither Brake nor White had noticed the little goblin. It needed to stay that way. She'd love to thank Bert for saving her, but doing it here would put him at risk.

White and Brake had stopped ahead, and she closed the distance and took a look at the wall blocking their progress. It wasn't a wall, or it wasn't *just* a wall, anyway. The surface was made from black slate, and a nearby tray held several pieces of brightly-colored chalk. A series of numbers had been emblazoned on the board, 13, 17, 19, 23. There was clearly room for a fifth number to be written afterward.

"What are we looking at, Master White?" the dwarf prompted. "Want me to try chopping through it?"

"No," White mused aloud. "I suspect that would only cause a magical explosion, one that we likely wouldn't survive. Kit, is this magical?"

Kit overrode the instinct the trope had implanted, though it took considerable effort not to chew out the necromancer for not casting the same spell he was asking her to use. She murmured a detect magic spell. "*Detecto magicus vice versa!*"

The board began to glow, a strong, steady blue of enchantment. The numbers bore a slightly different magical signature, and had transmutation blended in.

"The board is the doorway," she explained, leaning closer to inspect the enchantment. "If we insert the correct number, then it will open and we can proceed into the dark lord's lair."

"She's right," Sir Patrick's voice came from behind her, causing her to very nearly wet her pants. "If you can puzzle out the right series of numbers it will open the door. I've gotten past the first and the second, but have never beaten the third sequence. It's fairly typical. This is what I meant by the dark lord being mad. Kount loves numbers. He does *not* love interference, so I cannot help you solve this. Best of luck."

White eyed the knight crossly. "You've been supremely unhelpful so far."

"You're one to talk," Sir Patrick snapped. He stabbed a finger in White's direction. "Any self-respecting wizard should be able to solve the first two puzzles, at the very least. You think you're worthy of the title of lord? Prove it."

"You realize I could force you to commit suicide?" White's eyes narrowed. "I would take more care in what you say to me."

"Oh, no," Sir Patrick mimed, "don't kill me. Then I'll be dead. You have no leverage, necromancer. You can order me about, but you cannot still my tongue."

Kit was quite proud of the fact that she managed to hold hers. She'd never seen anyone take White down like that and sadly felt more kinship for the death knight than she did either White or Brakestuff. At least the knight had loyalties, and reasons to do things that went deeper than XP or loot.

White moved to the board and picked up a piece of chalk. He stared at the numbers, and stroked his goatee, coating it with blue chalk dust. "Hmm. This seems extremely complex." White stared at it for a while longer, until they all began to shift uncomfortably. His shoulders slumped, and he turned to Kit. "I'm a charisma-based caster, and the sequence is eluding me. No doubt only a true genius can decipher the pattern."

"Heh." Sir Patrick snorted a laugh. "True genius. Or your average fifth grader."

Kit walked over and calmly wrote the number 29 on the board. A peel of thunder sounded overhead, and the lights dimmed as thickly accented laugher came from all around them. "Ah, ah, ah. One. One puzzle beaten."

The lighting returned to normal.

"What did you do?" White asked as the blood drained from his face.

"They're prime numbers," she explained. It was so difficult not rubbing it in further, but she figured the best way to put this turd in his place was showing that she could succeed where he had failed. "Each number can only be divided by itself and 1. It's a fairly common problem, and one that's used often at Frogwarts, where I trained."

The board rippled, and four more numbers appeared, a 2, a 4, a 16, and a 256. Kit offered the chalk to White, but the necromancer waved her off. "While we're both equally capable of solving such challenges...you're already holding the chalk, and I feel it only fair to allow you to shine now and again."

Kit rolled her eyes as she turned back to the board, and wrote 65,536.

Again the thunder peeled overhead, and the thickly accented laugher came in its wake. "Ah, ah, ah. Two. Two puzzles beaten."

She didn't bother offering the chalk to White, but she did give him the same kind of condescending smile he so loved delivering. His face went psycho-killer blank, and she read her death in his eyes. Kit turned back to the board, and wished she'd made better life choices. How had she ended up with this guy?

The final sequence of numbers was tougher. A 21, 34, 55, and 89. "Hmm."

"You got this, kid." Brake patted her awkwardly.

Thanks to the well actually trope she did have it. She recognized the sequence, something that had terrified her back at university, until she'd realized how simple it was. "It's a Fibonacci sequence."

"Of course," White interjected. "I saw it immediately."

"What's a fibonok, or whatever?" the dwarf asked, peering up at White.

"Yes, White," she asked, horrified at herself even as she said the words. "Why don't you tell us what a Fibonacci sequence is?"

"I don't have time for this." He whirled away from her, and turned to the board.

Brakestuff tugged lightly on her robe to get her attention. "So like, what's the fib thing again?"

"It's the sum of the two previous numbers," she explained. "So one plus one is two, two plus one is three, two plus three is five, and so on. Make sense?"

The dwarf laughed. "Not even a little bit."

Kit wrote 144 on the board. A tremendous grinding began, and the door slid open. "Ah, ah, ah. Three. Three puzzles beaten. Come, join me in my throne room."

18

NUPPET

"Stupid necromancer, stealing credit." Bert glared at White as he trailed a ways behind the adventurers. He watched in awe as Kit performed some sort of magic on the board. He knew what numbers were, conceptually at least, but he'd always needed to use his fingers to count. If only he had more fingers.

Thunder cracked overhead a third time, and the wall slid open to reveal a passage into a dark room. A few torches flickered within, splashing their weak light on the dank stone.

The adventurers didn't hesitate, and plunged forward, the dwarf in the lead.

Bert patted his friend, and Lefty gently nudged him. Righty was asleep, of course. "Follow Bert. Stay in corner."

Boberton obediently followed Bert into the dark lord's chamber. It was depressingly normal, just a stone room with stone walls and a big, ugly, black throne in the back of the room. A terrifying vampire sat there, quite unlike the one that had attacked the adventurers back outside the magic shop.

This vampire wasn't nearly as tall, and in fact wasn't too much taller than Bert. The vampire wouldn't quite come up to the dwarf's shoulder. His clothing was very fancy, all black silks with scarlet lining. His jet-black hair was combed artfully down the middle, and he had a long, beak-like nose. Two long fangs protruded from his upper jaw, but he didn't seem to have any other teeth. His ears were long and curved, just like an elf.

Bert recognized the coarse texture of the violet skin. "Vampire made of rubber. Bert confused."

He didn't think that vampires could be made from rubber, and wondered what it was he was looking at. He turned to Kit, who stood in her elven form with her staff in hand, just behind White and Brake.

"What is it, Kit?" the dwarf roared, "and how do we fight it? Don't much resemble any vampire I've ever killed."

Kit's voice quavered a bit, in what Bert imagined must be fear. "That's no vampire. It's a nuppet. They're not undead. They're unliving. No one knows where they come from, though I believe they're from somewhere down near straggle rock, deep in the undersnark."

"Nuppets?" Brake asked. "Like Kermit the Slayer?"

"Exactly." Kit nodded. "Plan accordingly. They don't breathe, and have no heartbeat. The only way to beat one is overwhelming damage."

"That I can do." The dwarf gave a maniacal laugh, and charged the nuppet. The two went down in a tangle of limbs, but Bert had already lost interest.

"Come, Boberton." He began picking a path around the outer edge of the room, scanning for anything valuable.

He'd made it nearly halfway around the wall when he stopped and his jaw fell open. A huge pile of gold and gems sat directly behind the throne. Bert turned back to the adventurers, but they were all quite occupied with the dark lord.

Bert waddled across the room as fast as he could manage, and didn't stop until he stood next to the gold. There was so much of it.

He dropped his pack and flipped up the flap, then pulled out his trowel. Bert used it as a shovel, and heaped as many of the gems as he could into the bag. Gold coins slipped in as well, and before long he'd stuffed his bag until the seams bulged.

Bert waddled over to the straps, and tried picking up the bag. "Hhhnnnnngggg."

Nothing. He couldn't lift it. His eyes widened, and he turned to Boberton. "Can Boberton carry?"

Boberton wagged his tail eagerly.

Bert guided the dog down into a sitting position, and then slowwwwwly dragged the backpack toward the dog. It took fifteen or sixteen attempts to maneuver it into position, but he was able to get it cinched around the dog's shoulders.

Boberton stood up, and swayed a bit to the side, then righted himself. His tail wagged more fiercely than ever, despite the burden.

"Good dog." Boberton hugged his best friend. "Now follow Bert. Let's go back to monster shop. Buy Boberton fancy collar, and more pellets."

Bert turned and hurried from the room, Boberton trotting happily in his wake. No one seemed to notice, and he walked right out of the room. Then he walked back up the corridor, and through the chamber with the kittens. There was no sign of the mummy, and the kittens were afraid of Boberton.

Everything else he passed had been killed by the adventurers, and he didn't spy any threats as he made his way back to the main entry hall, which was still littered with corpses. He threaded a path through them, and stepped out onto the cobblestones.

He blinked a few times as his eyes adjusted to the brighter light. The sky was overcast, but still brighter than the tomb. It felt good to escape that place. He turned to Boberton, and hugged his best friend.

Bert couldn't believe it. He was rich. He could buy anything. He'd stolen the dark lord's treasure. That had to be enough to buy a warg.

19

AH, AH, AH

Thunder cracked overhead, and Kount studied them through his monocle. The tiny nuppet would probably only appear intimidating to someone like Bert, given how small and unassuming he was. But she knew that nuppets were terrifyingly lethal.

Kit watched the dark lord closely as she cast her haste spell. The magical energies washed over her friends, enhancing their speed. Kount didn't seem impressed.

The nuppet, despite his smaller size, flung Brakestuff into the wall with bone-shattering force, and the dwarf slumped to the ground. The nuppet followed up with a wicked roundhouse, and his tiny foot slammed into the dwarf's face in a spray of blood.

Then Kount's hands moved in a blur, and his fists rock-eted into the dwarf's face over and over and over. "Ah, ah, ah. Seven. Seven punches to your ugly face." Thunder crashed overhead, high outside the tomb.

Kount flipped up and away just in time to avoid Sir Patrick's massive sword, which whistled through the space the nuppet had just occupied. The Kount landed on the edge of the knight's sword, and ran up its length, then plunged both small hands into Sir Patrick's eyes, temporarily blinding him. "One, two. Two eyes blinded."

"No," Sir Patrick roared. He dropped his sword and started swinging wildly with his fists. "I'm mostly blind, but I can still see lights."

"How many are there?" Kount demanded. He flipped back from the death knight, apparently distracted by the need to count.

Sir Patrick blinked his glowing eyes, and peered around the room. "Three, no four. There are four lights. I'm certain of it."

"Ah, ah, ah," Kount began thrusting a hand at the first torch. "One, two, three, four lights. There are four lights." Thunder crashed outside again.

White hadn't been idle and aimed his rod of undead domination at the nuppet. The skull at the end loosed a beam of black energy, but the Kount pivoted and interposed his monocle. The beam was reflected back at White, knocking him back a step.

"Damn it," White cursed. He turned to Brake. "Get up, and end that thing. You're losing to a nuppet. You should be embarrassed."

Kit wished there were something more she could do. Since she wasn't allowed to learn combat spells, all she could do was buff her party members, and casting something like an enlarge spell on Brake would only make it harder for him to catch the slippery nuppet.

She rooted around in her pack, and looked at the seals to all the spells she'd bought.

"Kit!" White gave a panicked shriek as Kount started in his direction. "Fireball it. Paralyze it. Do something!"

Kit reached the highest level scroll, or one of them at

least. Phantasmal killer. She knew what the spell did, in theory. It would summon a phantom to kill the target. That phantom would appear real, and if the target believed in the spell, then they died. Cunning targets who suspected the illusion shrugged off the effects. She could try using it, but had no idea if it would even affect a nuppet, much less one who'd risen to dark lord.

Brake shot to his feet and sprinted at Kount. He tackled the nuppet from behind, and the two rolled end over end across the stone.

Kit cast without thinking, giving Brake a bull's strength spell in the hopes that he might come out on top this time. It didn't help.

Kount's leg scythed out, and caught Brake in the jaw. Kount head-butted the dwarf, who rolled off him with a groan. The dark lord flipped to his feet and sprinted after White. Kit reached for the phantasmal killer scroll, but hesitated for a moment. This was a chance to let Kount finish off White, and the world might be better for that.

No, she couldn't desert a companion. Kit cracked the seal on the scroll and began to read, "*Raucisonos efflabant cornua!*"

Mist swirled on the ground near her feet, just to the right. It bubbled and frothed, until a pair of ghostly hands appeared, and a person pulled themselves free. The spell had summoned an incorporeal man in archaic clothing, which hung in tattered remains around an emaciated form.

"I am Wilhelm the Banshee," the specter proudly proclaimed. "Why have you summoned me, wizard? Who must I slay?"

"Kill Dark Lord Kount!" She pointed at the nuppet, and prayed that this spell would work. If it didn't, she was fresh out of answers. Maybe Bert could somehow save them again.

"You might want to cover your ears," Wilhelm cautioned. "My scream is quite deadly."

The banshee floated toward the dark lord, and unleashed a warbling scream. She covered her ears, and still winced from the secondary impact. Being the primary target must be infinitely worse.

Kount spun to face his attacker. The rubber along his face had begun to bubble and melt, and ran down like waxy tears. He sprinted toward the banshee, but just before Kount arrived Brake tackled him from behind, for the third time.

"Hit him again!" the dwarf roared.

Wilhelm screamed again. More of Kount's face bubbled away. Wilhelm screamed again, and again, while the dwarf kept him pinned in place. All in all, it was rather anticlimactic. The poor nuppet struggled to free himself, but he really had no chance.

After a fifth scream the nuppet twitched a final time, and then his melted body went limp. Brake hurled him into the wall, and Kount slid down into a limp pile.

"That seemed too easy," Kit muttered.

"You're right," White agreed. He rose to his feet, and straightened his jaw with a free hand. "If Kount had the dark lord trope he should be effectively immortal. I don't understand how he was killed by a fourth level spell."

Wilhelm gave a scandalized squawk, and then flowed into a pile of mist and disappeared. He was an effective, if touchy, ghost.

Kit moved to squat next to Kount's discarded body. She gasped, and looked up to meet White's gaze. "His trope socket had this." She plucked a small purple stone from the socket. "I recognize it. It's the Mad Counter trope. Useless, unless you want to hear some thunder."

"Then where is the dark lord trope?" White roared, his face going splotchy.

"Probably in his treasure trove, I'd imagine." She shrugged. "I guess we start by searching this place."

White gave a reluctant nod, more in control now. "Yes, that's good. We'll search this place and see what we find. Fan out, and see what you can locate. I want that trope."

Each of them moved in a different direction, slowly circling walls and inspecting pillars as they sought secret compartments or hidden gems.

"Over here," Brake called. He was standing next to the throne.

Kit hurried over to join him, and craned around to see what he was looking at behind the throne. A few dozen gold pieces were scattered across the floor, and a couple rubies, but nothing else. Certainly no dark lord trope.

"So let me see if I understand this," Brake growled. "We killed the dark lord and not only do we not get his trope, but he has no treasure? Was this guy broke? Where did it go?"

Kit smiled into her hand as White rushed over to inspect the meager remains. She had a feeling she knew exactly who'd made off with the treasure. Somehow it seemed fitting, especially since they wouldn't have let her keep anything interesting anyway.

Good for Bert.

20

MONSTER SHOP II

B ert and Boberton picked their way back down the hill, which hadn't much changed in their absence. The sky was still steel grey. Clusters of skeletal guards still stood at most street corners. People kept their heads down, and moved quickly to wherever they were going.

No one paid any attention to Bert, but he still encouraged Boberton to plod along as quickly as he could manage with the heavy pack. The dog didn't complain, but Bert could see how hard the pup was struggling with the weight.

It took a long time to make it all the way back to the monster shop, and by that point Boberton's legs were beginning to wobble. "It's okay, boy. Almost there."

Bert found a discarded branch, which he used to force the door's handle down. It popped open, and Bert guided Boberton inside. He brought the heavily laden dog to the counter, and then quickly helped the dog out of the pack. Lefty gave Bert several enthusiastic licks, then settled down to sleep next to Righty.

The chair was still where Bert had left it, so he scrambled up and waited for the shopkeeper to notice him. The old man heard the chair leg scrape the floor, and peered down his spectacles. "Oh, it's you, young fella! Bert, wasn't it? I see you made it back. That was faster than I expected."

"Bert rich," he explained. Bert proudly flipped the top of his pack open and exposed the gold and gems inside. Several glittering stones toppled out, and he gave a horrified squawk, then dropped down to collect them.

Only, one of the gems that had fallen out wasn't a gem. It was a trope, and not just any trope, but a shiny, black one that was cold to the touch. Bert hadn't noticed it when he'd been shoveling loot into the bag. He turned it over and studied the symbol on it, a skeleton with a crown sitting on a big throne that looked a lot like the dark lord's.

"Hmm." Bert stuffed the trope into his pocket. He'd add it to his notebook later. He gathered the rest of the coins and gems, and then clambered back up to put them on the counter. "Bert want to buy dire wolf."

The shopkeeper gave Bert the widest, friendliest grin anyone had ever beamed in his direction. "Well, all right then. I don't know how you pulled it off, but good on you. Why don't you let me take the gold? You can hang on to the gems, which shouldn't burden your dog so. How's he working out by the way?"

"Boberton?" Bert perked up and stared down at the little dog. "Boberton great. Bert really love. Thank you." He smiled down at his sleeping friend. Boberton let out a long, low fart that caused the wood on the counter to buckle and crack.

"Ack." The shopkeeper blinked away tears. "Those magic pellets sure have a kick. Smells like a dead animal ate another dead animal, then died again. Let's head out back to collect your mount."

Bert hopped down off the chair, and gently roused Boberton. Lefty woke up, and the dog's tail began to thump weakly. "Boberton, going outside. Want to go with Bert, or stay here?"

Boberton hopped to his feet. He'd regained his energy, even though he'd only been asleep for a few moments. Bert wished he could recover that quickly.

They followed the shopkeeper down a narrow hallway, which led to the opposite side of the building from where he'd picked up Boberton.

The hallway ended in a yard, which was lined with several very large pens. Bert passed a G. Scorpion, which waved its stinger and clacked its claws as if showing off what it could do. Beyond it stood the answer to every one of Bert's prayers and hopes.

A massive grey wolf lounged in a cell, its enormous snout resting between paws that could smother Bert. It had to be twice as large as Head Warg Rider's mount. Everyone in town would take him seriously, if he came in riding this beauty.

"What wolf's name?" Bert wondered aloud.

"He doesn't have one." The shopkeeper gave an apologetic shrug. "He's just a generic dire wolf. It's a mount, not a pet. He ain't too bright, but he'll serve you loyally, if you keep him fed."

"Oh." Bert's shoulders slumped. He was sort of hoping to make another friend. "If Bert names him will he learn name?"

The shopkeeper shook his head. "Even odds he won't. He might, but I can't promise he will. It's like with a dog. Some are smarter than others. Hard to say."

"Oh. Can Bert meet?" Bert walked over to the front of the pen, and the dire wolf gave him a disinterested sniff.

"Course, son." The old man unlatched the cage, and gestured for Bert to step inside.

Bert waddled into the pen. "Wolf okay with Bert climbing on top?"

The wolf merely watched him, but Bert assumed that meant yes. He walked over, and clambered up the wolf's side. By the time he reached the beast's back he was out of breath. "Long climb. Very high up."

Bert imagined himself as part of a war charge, riding into battle atop his mighty steed, against the feral cats. He imagined the wind, and all the other goblins cheering and calling his name. Bert's smile grew and grew. He couldn't believe he'd finally done it.

A quiet whine came from below, and Bert looked down to find Boberton staring up at him. Lefty looked up at Bert, then very pointedly looked at his back, then looked back at Bert.

"Ohhh," Bert realized aloud. "Boberton not want Bert to buy new mount?"

Boberton gave another whine, and began racing back and forth outside the pen, barking.

Bert rested his hands in his lap. He stared down at the wolf, which hadn't really reacted to his presence. It wasn't a friend, and it wouldn't ever be. It was just a...vehicle, really. A way to get around. Before that might have been okay. But now that he'd learned what friends were? Boberton was the better choice.

"Okay, okay." Bert clambered back down the side of the wolf, which was far enough that he got a little dizzy. Boberton was waiting just outside the pen. "Bert will wait until Boberton is large enough to ride." He patted the dog, and Lefty eagerly licked his hand.

"You're making a smart move, son, if you ask me. That

dog clearly loves you." The shopkeeper nodded approvingly, and then closed the pen. "Tell you what. You want to stay here for a day or two while you figure out how to spend that coin, I'm happy to have you. I've got an extra room, now that my boy moved on to Frogwarts. What do you say?"

"Okay." Bert raised a hand, and grabbed the shopkeeper's index finger so they could shake. "Bert happy to pay for room. And for mess Boberton makes."

The shopkeeper laughed at that. "Son, I think we're gonna get along just great."

21

THE WHITE TOWER

K it found the day after the death of the dark lord a strange one. The party scoured the entire tomb searching for loot, but found surprisingly little that they could sell. The Kount had a love of books, which Kit appreciated, but apparently not of gold. Whatever treasure had been here had, presumably, been behind the throne and now belonged to the mysterious thief.

Kit fervently hoped that thief was Bert, as the mere idea of the goblin having that amount of money to spend was hilarious. The idea that he might have the dark lord trope was a good deal less so. What if he sold it to a merchant, who sold it to someone smart enough to understand how powerful it was? What if he followed another adventuring party, and someone like White got ahold of it?

She needed to find Bert, but before she could do that Kit needed to tend to a gigantic problem. A problem so gigantic that 'Master White' was having trouble fitting it through doorways. That problem, of course, was his ego.

Kit strode into the throne room, where White had been spending most of his time. He lounged there now, thumbing through one of several necromantic tomes they'd recovered from Kount. White glanced up at her entrance, his robes even more badly stained than they'd been before. If anything they were more brown now than white, and in the right light could pass for black.

"Ah, Kit, you came." White threw his leg over the arm of the throne, a blatant 'look at me and how powerful I am' kind of move. "Please, stand in the corner and do not speak."

Kit was used to White's outrageous requests, and stifled her trope's impulse to verbally flay the bastard. Doing so would only make her situation worse. "Why did you invite me here if you don't want my counsel? I thought this was a meeting to decide the fate of the tomb. I helped you clear it. I have a say in what happens to it."

"No, you don't." White rose from the throne, and ambled over to her, a condescending smile slipping into place. He waved a finger directly under her nose, but Kit stood her ground. "You have no say. No opinion. Not of worth, anyway. Brake and I have called the OLP here to decide, collectively, what is to be done with this place. You don't use white magic. You have no place in that decision."

"So again," Kit growled, as her nails dug into her palms. If only she could afford to offend this bastard, "why did you ask me here?"

"Oh." White seemed to relax, and returned to his throne. "I asked you here to provide refreshments. The Kount kept a fully stocked larder. If any of the wizards require butterbeer, or wine, or hash hish or what have you, then you will procure it. The Kount kept an impressive collection. Apparently he was quite the connoisseur."

Again, Kit forced a deep breath. How had she been so badly outmaneuvered? When they'd began this, White had just been another party member. Now, though, he'd seized control of the group, and through it likely this entire kingdom. Kit had no doubt that inviting the council here was merely a formality. He wanted the wizards to kiss the ring, so to speak.

"Who else did you invite?" She moved to stand near White's throne. It was possible he might have summoned someone she could make common cause with. Not likely though. White was too canny for that.

"You'll see." White straightened on his throne, and spent a moment fixing his hair. It seemed laughable when his robes were so grimy. Even upwind of his musk she still gagged a little.

Steps sounded outside the throne room, slow and deliberate. They paused, then continued, then paused, then continued. After a few minutes an old man lurched into the room. He leaned heavily on a thick oaken staff, and had a long, white beard that nearly brushed the stone. A wide-brimmed, conical hat, bent and battered, perched atop his head.

"Announce them," White hissed out of the corner of his mouth.

Kit was about to give White the worst tongue lashing of his life. He'd assumed she'd just know who his guests were? Only, she did know. This one was unmistakable, and since she knew, she may as well go along with White rather than deal with his tantrum. "May I present Gondeaf the White."

"What? Speak up, young lady." The wizard mopped sweat from his forehead, and moved to lean against the wall. "So...many...stairs."

"If you used real magic," came a British voice, as cultured as it was measured, "you wouldn't need stairs." Another elderly white man stepped through a vertical slash in the air, and his beard did brush the stone. Like Gondeaf, his robes were a snowy white, though of a slightly different style. The only thing that really distinguished him was a jaunty hat with a little tassel, and the braid that tied the middle of his beard.

"May I present," Kit announced, as solemnly as she had the first time, "Bumbledork, Headmaster of Frogwarts Magical University."

She'd never spoken directly with the headmaster during her time at school, and was no less comfortable under the weight of his attention now that she was a full-fledged sorceress.

"What?" Gondeaf demanded, cupping his hand to his ear. "He said something rude about me, didn't he?"

Bumbledork moved to the wall opposite Gondeaf, and scowled. The pair's rivalry was well known, and Kit thought White was playing with fire having both here. There might be something there she could exploit.

More steps sounded outside, these heavy and metallic. Brakestuff strode into the room, a tankard clutched in one gauntleted hand. He raised it to White, then moved to stand next to Kit. "Master White."

"Welcome, old friend." White turned to address the group. "We await only one more arrival, and then we can get started."

Kit realized that another person was abruptly standing in the room. One moment he was not there, and the next he was. This last wizard looked nearly identical to the other two. Same beard, similar robes, and a wooden staff to complete the ensemble. Only his lack of a hat distinguished him.

She wasn't a hundred percent sure who it was, at first. She could rule out Oz, as he didn't have a beard. But it could have been Elminister, from the barely remembered realms. There were just so many white wizards with long beards and wooden staves. Then she realized who it must be.

"May I present," she intoned, "Merlin of Camelatte."

"Welcome, welcome," White called from the throne, magnanimously of course. "Thank you all for coming, gentlemen. You represent the finest sorcerers and wizards this world has to offer. There is more magical talent in this room than in the rest of the world combined, and I feel that's a humble assessment."

All three of the wizards preened a bit at that.

"I've asked you here to discuss a grave threat to the land." White's face took on a concerned expression, one she had no doubt he'd practiced for hours. "My companions and I barely overcame the sitting dark lord. He was powerful, but we bested him."

"Grats on that," Merlin said. The other two muttered their congratulations as well.

"Thank you, thank you." White gave a smug wave. "We would give anything to help others, just as you yourselves would. I called you here because a threat still remains. The dark lord did not possess the trope. It was stolen, perhaps some time ago. That means it is out in the wild, gentlemen. Out there where anything could find it. Imagine if a dragon or a lich recovered that trope. They could make an army that would make the world tremble."

All three men gave grave nods, even Gondeaf, who clearly had no idea what was being said.

"What do you propose to do about it?" Bumbledork asked. The way he asked it suggested the answer was obvious, but that he wanted White, with his limited intellect, to puzzle it out for himself.

Kit was amazed this much smugness could fit into a

single room.

"The answer is simple, gentlemen." White leaned forward on his throne. "We band together, and eradicate all evil in the land. If there are no monsters, then we need not fear another dark lord. Let us make this world safe for its citizens."

Kit failed to stifle her eye roll, but thankfully no one seemed to notice. She wondered if White bought his own bullshit. She doubted it.

"You want to bring this place under the protection of the OLP?" Merlin asked in his vaguely disinterested tone, which was remarkably similar to Bumbledork's.

"Something like that," White explained. "We are all white wizards, yes?"

Again everyone nodded.

"Then I propose we declare this the White Tower, and as I am the one who has liberated it, that we bestow stewardship of this place to me."

It all sounded so reasonable. Even Kit couldn't think of a protest, though not for lack of trying. The idea of White unifying these people into one force terrified her. The OLP could do a lot of damage, collectively.

Bumbledork fiddled with his beard. "I'll second the motion."

"Third," Brakestuff immediately supplied. "And I'll second White being placed in charge. We can trust him. He's lawful good."

The motion passed unanimously, though Kit doubted Gondeaf had any idea what he was voting for. Everything White had done seemed logical, and she couldn't argue that having the dark lord trope in the wild wasn't dangerous.

But she feared the power White would seize in the name of hunting it.

22

GARBAGE

Bert woke up with a stretch and a yawn. He blinked sleepily around him and realized he was on the softest bed he'd ever slept on. It was large enough for two big humans, or about forty goblins. Bert had most of it to himself, except for the large, warm lump next to him.

Boberton gave competing snores from both Lefty and Righty. Bert wriggled out from under the big dog, and noted that Boberton was larger than when he'd gone to sleep. The dog was already bigger than Bert, and growing more so every day. He had a rough, earthy smell to him that Bert was quickly growing fond of. It was a marked contrast to the other smells Boberton was capable of.

Righty gave a snort, and his eyes blinked open. Bert tensed, ready to dive off the side of the bed if the dog started barking. Righty blinked one more time, and gave a quiet woof. That seemed to wake Lefty, and as soon as both heads were awake the dog excitedly hopped down off the bed and turned in a small circle.

"Bert coming." Bert moved to the corner of the bed, and began climbing down the post. It took a bit to reach the ground, but sleeping on something that soft was worth it. "Okay, Boberton. We've got big day. Let's go talk to shopkeeper."

The floorboards creaked as Bert waddled across them. He'd left the door open since unlatching it would have been impractical, and walked out and into the shop's main room. The kindly shopkeeper was already behind his counter, humming happily to himself while he straightened a series of books on a little shelf.

"Oh, good morning, Bert." The shopkeeper smiled his way. "So today's the big day, huh?"

Bert nodded eagerly as he hurried over to the counter. "Bert ready. Going to make goblin history. Bert richest goblin ever."

The shopkeeper gave a hearty laugh, then came out from around the corner. "If you look out front I've left you a little present. I've got a rickety old cart I was meaning to throw out, and since you're going to the dump anyway I figure you can use it to carry your pack."

"Oh. Thank you." Bert clapped excitedly. "Perfect. Pack really heavy."

Since he hadn't bought the warg he still had a large amount of gold, and even though Boberton was growing fast Bert didn't think it fair to ask the dog to carry it all the way to the dump. As he understood it the dump was on the far side of town, all the way up a big hill.

"You're doing me a favor, really." The old man moved to the shop door, and hefted the crossbeam out of the way, then pushed the door open. "There we go. On your way now, son. You've got big things to do, sounds like."

Bert hurried over the threshold, and gave his new friend a final wave. He found it odd that the shopkeeper didn't have a name, but the man claimed he didn't need a name to sell monsters.

Sure enough a large wooden cart sat a few feet from the door. Its four wheels were warped and worn, and the slats making up the wagon were faded and cracked. It was the most beautiful wagon Bert had ever seen, because it was his.

He waddled over and removed the pack from Boberton, then heaved and pulled, and heaved until he was able to maneuver it into his cart. Then he turned to Boberton, who stood expectantly a couple feet away.

"Boberton, will you pull wagon?" Bert asked. He fetched a ball of twine from his bag, and began to fix the wagon's rod to the dog's collar.

Boberton perked up, and Lefty gave a proud bark. Righty went to sleep.

"Good dog." Bert patted Boberton's side which was getting harder to do since the dog was taller now. "Pull wagon up hill." Bert pointed toward the hill at the far side of town, which nestled against the big mountains Bert had made his way around.

He knew that right on the other side of that hill lay Paradise.

Boberton started in that direction, and the two snaked their way across the city. It was early enough that there wasn't much foot traffic, but what little Bert did see was both interesting and useful.

Several carts drawn by teams of mules were making their way through the city. Most buildings had left a large bin of trash on their curb, and the carts would pull up to each house, and dump the refuse into their wagons. In exchange, the mules would poop in the street outside the houses. Perhaps the poop was valuable for some reason.

The wagons, once full, made their way up the cobblestone road on the eastern hill. Bert hurried after the closest one, and followed it up the same streets. Boberton expertly avoided the mule droppings, and Righty kept darting concerned glances at the cart.

"Good dog," Bert affirmed. And he meant it. "Boberton very good at pulling cart. Much better than mules."

Boberton walked a little taller.

They followed the cart, and rested each time it picked up refuse, which made the trip much less exhausting than it otherwise would have been. Humans were accustomed to walking many miles a day, but goblins had very small legs, and Bert could only go so far before he needed to lay down for a while.

As they made their way up the hill Bert had his first good look at the lift used to haul garbage. It was ingenious. A large team of mules were roped to some sort of crank, and as the crank turned, a large, flat lift was carried to the top of the mountain. When it reached the top, a group of workers hurried onto the lift and began throwing things over the side.

Bert was very thoughtful as they continued up the hill. The carts were, not surprisingly, making their way toward the lift. A small building squatted to the left of the lift, its windows covered under a layer of impenetrable grime.

"Bert bet person who own garbage inside." He started waddling in that direction.

23

MASTER GARBOLOGIST

Bert tugged Boberton over to the small building, and parked the cart outside. He patted the dog, and considered whether he should bring the pack inside. No, it would be fine for a few minutes. "Boberton watch cart."

Boberton stood at attention, and turned in a slow circle as Lefty scanned for threats. Finding nothing, he sat back on his haunches, and started scratching an itch on his side. Bert was satisfied.

He headed over to the building, and breathed easier when he realized the door was already open. There was no way he could reach the latch, which sat a little higher than it did on most human doors.

Bert cautiously peered inside, and saw a woman nearly as wide as she was tall standing next to a window with a coffee pot in her hand. She finished filling a mug, then stirred in some cream as she muttered to herself under her breath. Bert caught something about Mondays, but since he didn't know what 'mon' was, it wasn't clear why she would hate the days with it.

The woman's overalls bore a variety of interesting stains, the telltale sign of a master garbologist. This woman had seen a lot of trash.

Bert withdrew his little cap, and held it in both hands as he waddled up to the woman. She didn't seem to notice him. *Hmm.* He brightened, reached into his pocket, and removed the wrapper from yesterday's sandwich. Bert crumped it into a tight ball, and tossed it in front of the woman.

Her eyes locked onto the piece of garbage, and she squatted down to examine it. "Hmm, mustard stain. Got a baloney smell to it, too. Wonder how it got here?"

Bert walked over and stood next to the wrapper. "Hello." He extended a hand, just like all the humans seemed to do.

The woman blinked a few times, and then brushed some copper-colored curls out of her eyes. "Well, I'll be. You're a critter who can talk. Don't see that too often."

"Me Bert," he eloquently explained. "Bert here for business. Bert have gold. Want to buy garbage."

The woman just stared at him for several long moments, and then stood up. She took a sip from her coffee, and stared down at him fixedly with one eye. "Let me see if I got this straight. You want to pay me—in gold, mind—to buy some garbage? You've certainly got my attention. Normally other people pay me to pick up the garbage and haul it off. Never considered it might have some extra value. In fact, our biggest expense is hauling it up the mountain and dumping it over the side."

Bert was stunned into speechlessness. He couldn't wrap his brain around the concept. Other people paid this woman to haul their garbage away? They paid to get rid of it when they could be selling it. The beginnings of an idea began to take root.

"You dump garbage over side of hill, right? Down into Paradise?" He pointed in the direction of the goblin town.

"Paradise?" The woman gave a snort and set her coffee down on the window ledge. "Ohhh...I get it. You're a goblin. You must be talking about the goblin settlement down at the edge of the dump. So, your little buddies like garbage? Enough to pay for it?"

Bert nodded eagerly. "Bert have idea. Instead of dumping garbage from top of lift, charge goblins—"

"These goblins got gold?"

Bert's shoulders slumped as he spotted the enormous flaw in his plan. "No. Only Bert have gold."

"Well don't get yer knickers in a twist now." She beamed a gap-toothed smile down at him. "You and Stella can still work a deal, I think."

Bert thought about that. His mom liked garbage. Everyone did, even G. Mayor. But the only thing they could pay with was other garbage. He couldn't make a profitable business that way.

"Wait, people pay Stella to collect trash, right?" Bert had another idea.

"That they do. Enough to get by, though not with much to spare." She picked up her coffee again, and stared wistfully out the window. "Truth is this place barely runs. Used to be that the old king supported us with a subsidy, but when the dark lord came to power all that stopped."

"How much gold to buy whole business?" Bert asked.

"What?" She blinked down at him, then planted her hands on her hips. "You having a go at me?" She gave an eye roll, but also a smile. "All right then, tell you what. You pay me a thousand gold pieces and this place is all yours."

"Okay," Bert immediately agreed. He thrust out his hand again. "Stella and Bert make deal."

"All right then." She skeptically lowered a hand, and Bert seized a finger and shook. "You bring back the gold and this place is all yours."

"Bert be right back." He started for the door, but stopped before he reached it. The ideas just kept coming, and this one he didn't want to forget. "How much to have Stella stay and help Bert?"

Stella gave an amused grunt. "Since we're dreaming, tell you what, you make it fifteen hundred gold and I'll stay on and run the place as long as you want."

"Okay." Bert turned and headed for the door. He waddled out to the cart, and was impressed to find Boberton sitting at attention. Even Righty was awake. "Boberton, bring cart inside. We give lady gold."

The dog's tiny tail began to wag, and it hurried over to the door. Bert helped Boberton navigate with the cart, and then parked it in front of the counter. Bert clambered up onto the cart, which swayed alarmingly. He opened the flap, and began removing rolls of gold pieces. Bert stacked them on the counter, one after another.

Stella walked over and picked up the first one, then peeled back a corner of the roll. Her jaw fell open, and her toothpick clattered to the ground. "You got a name, partner? Cause it looks like you and I are in business."

"Bert." He jerked a thumb at himself. "My name Bert." He dumped a small sack of rubies on the counter, then started grabbing more gold.

"Okay, but from now on how about I call you 'boss,' since you own all this?" She gestured at the building and the lift outside.

Bert smiled. He liked the sound of boss.

24

RETURN TO PARADISE

B ert refastened Boberton's harness, and climbed into his newly modified wagon. Stella had pointed out that since he owned the place he could take any of the garbage waiting to be dumped, and Bert had spent the previous afternoon collecting a small pile of boards, wire, and a good-sized washbasin.

He'd reinforced the axle with a sturdy board, and used wire to fix the washbasin atop the wagon. That had meant removing the aging wooden sides, which Bert had converted into rope ladders that dangled over the side so he could easily climb in and out.

"Okay, Boberton. Let's go home." Bert climbed up the ladder, and heaved himself into the washbasin. He moved to the prow, and climbed atop the barstool he'd installed.

Bert reached down and picked up his fishing rod, then dangled the line in front of Boberton. He'd affixed one of Boberton's magic pellets to the hook on the end, and dangled it a few feet in front of the dog.

Boberton happily plodded down the trail, which snaked into the valley below. Paradise lay all the way at the bottom, and normally this would be an exhausting hike. Boberton and the wagon didn't just make it easier. They made it fun.

The wind whistled past them, and Bert gave a whoop of joy as Boberton picked up speed. He was so glad he hadn't gotten the warg. This was much better.

After about fifteen minutes of staring down at the approaching village, dreaming about what people would say about his awesome new vehicle, Bert let Boberton catch the pellet. Lefty eagerly wolfed it down, and Bert pulled the rod back to add another pellet to the line.

To his surprise, Boberton started down the path without needing the incentive. The dog seemed to realize where they were going, and made unerringly for Paradise.

Bert relaxed, and pulled out the sack lunch Stella had graciously provided for him. He liked that word, 'graciously.' He needed to find some situations to work it into conversation. "Bert graciously give Boberton pellet."

He fished out a wrapped sandwich, a light-colored bread with some sort of tasty white meat and a layer of cheese. Bert inhaled deeply, and then shoved the entire sandwich into his mouth. He spent the next few minutes blissfully chewing as Boberton guided them down the trail, little puffs of dust going up in their wake.

By the time they reached the valley floor the sun had crested the mountains, and Bert nervously eyed the town. He'd expected it to take less time, and now he was running out. He needed everyone to be at the garbage field by noon, or they'd miss his big demonstration.

Bert considered urging Boberton to greater speed, but really had no idea how to do that. Or how to ask him to stop. *Hmm*, perhaps he should have thought this through a bit more. Bert leaned on the edge of the washbasin, toward the dog. "Boberton, stop!"

Boberton obediently slowed to a stop, and turned expectantly to watch Bert. Amazing. How much of what he said did the dog understand? A great deal, it seemed.

"Boberton, go!"

The dog leapt into motion.

"Wow, Boberton smart." Bert gave an elated cheer. "Boberton, go faster!"

The dog redoubled his trot, and they ate up the last few hundred feet to the valley floor. Boberton hurried toward the village, the cart bumping along in his wake. Bert had, quite literally, never been happier.

The cart rumbled along, and before long they grew close enough to Paradise for the warg riders to spot them. Head Warg Rider lazily mounted his warg, and began to ride over, several other warg riders in his wake. Even the wargs swaggered, a swagger that Bert had always admired.

Now though? Now he had Boberton. They could keep their wargs.

Boberton hurried up to the closest warg, his tail wagging double time as he pulled the cart along. He sniffed at the warg and gave a welcoming woof, but the warg turned away and didn't even look at Boberton.

"Bert back," Head Warg Rider teased, as if that were somehow an insult. "Where you find stupid wagon, and stupid dog? Dog broken. Have two heads."

All the warg riders laughed cruelly, and so did some of the wargs. Boberton's tail drooped.

Sudden rage bubbled up in Bert. How dare they be mean to Boberton, who was worth ten of their wargs? "Head Warg Rider think he smart. He not smart. You come to garbage field when sun high in sky, and Bert show you that Bert way smarter than you."

"Why? Tomorrow garbage day. Not today. Nothing

happen today. Bert stupid." The warg riders started laughing again.

"Then come to field," Bert taunted. "Bert will show you who stupid."

He already felt the pressure on his head from being around other goblins, but it hadn't impacted him too heavily yet. He took a deep breath, and focused on Boberton. "Come on, Boberton. Let's go see G. Mayor."

Bert unfurled his rope ladder, and climbed down to the ground. He moved to join Boberton, and beckoned the dog. "This way, Boberton."

The dog's tail came up, and he started trotting after Bert, the cart rumbling in his wake. Righty had slept through the whole thing, but Lefty still looked a little sad. "Don't mind them. Warg riders stupid. Boberton is best mount ever."

Boberton once again straightened, and Bert smiled. He wanted his friend to be proud of himself. The dog was smarter than most goblins, and smelled way better, when he wasn't farting at least.

They reached the town center, where the junk buildings were taller, and more precarious. G. Mayor was trying to erect a new wing to his house, but was pulling materials from the upper floors to do it. The whole three-story building swayed with every gust of wind, and Bert was careful to keep Boberton out of the path should the building fall.

"G. Mayor!" Bert yelled. He brightened when the mayor turned in his direction. One positive of being back in town was that everyone could see him. "Bert have news. Bert garbologist now."

Bert hurried closer to G. Mayor, Boberton trotting in his wake. The disgruntled elder goblin turned to face Bert, his wrinkled skin settling into grey-green folds around a pair of beady eyes. He gave a weary sigh. "Bert home. More pieces of metal, Bert?"

"Uh, no." Bert looked back at his wagon. He did have a lot of pieces of metal left, gold metal, but G. Mayor wouldn't care. He turned back to the goblin. "Bert have news. Bert bought dump from humies. Bert own all garbage now."

"Bert crazy." G. Mayor rolled his eyes, but he came down from his house and walked over. "What Bert rattling about? G. Mayor working."

Bert considered the best way to go about this. G. Mayor wouldn't believe him. He needed to see it. Bert gazed skyward, and realized that he only had a half hour or so until the garbage came down.

"Tomorrow garbage day, right?" Bert asked.

"Right." G. Mayor wore his suspicion openly. "What point?"

"Garbage will come today," Bert proudly predicted. "Bert own garbage now. Proof come soon. You'll see."

G. Mayor gave an undignified huff. "Bert crazy." He turned back to his construction, and Bert sighed.

He wasn't going to get the mayor to come. He didn't really care if the villagers came, but he did care what his mother thought. She wouldn't believe him either, but he might be able to drag her out to see.

Bert hurried home, Boberton in tow. A few goblins shot him looks as he passed, but no one hassled him. That was a noticeable improvement. They were too curious about his wagon, or about the dog pulling it.

"Boberton, wait here." Bert stopped outside his mother's warren. There was no way Boberton would fit inside. "Be back soon. With mom."

Bert patted the dog, and Lefty licked his cheek. Bert giggled, then turned to his mother's warren and began worming his way through the garbage tunnels. They'd shifted since the last time he'd been here, and he had to backtrack twice before he reached his mother's sitting room.

"Mom?" he called as he entered.

"Bert!" She rose from her chair, a deep scowl spreading. "Where Bert go?"

"Bert have adventure," he proclaimed, standing like he imagined a hero might stand, arms raised. "Bert own all the garbage now. Bert tell humies to send today."

His mother eyed him suspiciously. She walked over, seized his head in both hands, and inspected inside his ears. "Don't see bugs. Seems like Bert okay. Why talk crazy?"

"Come see," Bert begged. "Bert can prove."

"Fine." She acquiesced. "But if Bert wrong..." The unspoken threat was more chilling than anything she could have said.

She grabbed a threadbare jacket from the peg on the wall and draped it over her like a cloak. Bert helped her into the tunnel, then dutifully followed while she crawled out of the warren. She picked a short path, and before long they were back outside.

"Mom." Bert touched her arm and pointed at his best friend. "Meet Boberton. Boberton meet mom. Boberton will take us to garbage field."

His mother moved to stand next to Boberton, and stared critically up at him. Lefty stared down at her in abject terror, and a runnel of yellow liquid rolled out from under the dog. Righty awakened with a snort, and blinked a few times before his gaze settled on Bert's mother.

Righty scooted forward and gave her a single lick on the cheek.

"Hmm." Mother turned back to Bert, and her expression softened a hair. "Dog good. Like dog. Good job, Bert."

Bert hurried over to the rope ladder. "This way!"

He helped his mother up, then clambered up after her. When he'd reached the top he moved to his barstool, but his mother was already sitting there. Bert squeezed around her, and jumped up to grab the lip of the washbasin. He pulled himself high enough to see over it, "Boberton, go to field with garbage."

Boberton gave a pair of nods, then started trotting over to the dump, where most goblins made their livelihood. Dozens of pairs of curious eyes looked up as they passed and Bert couldn't help but grin at the jealous whispers.

No one had a cart with a mount to pull it, not even the warg riders.

A gasp came from his mother, and Bert frantically followed her gaze. She was looking at the cliff, at the place where the living garbage came from. Garbage had begun to rain down, exactly one day early, as Bert had predicted. He swelled with pride, and looked up at his mother.

She smiled down at him. "Bert not total waste. Make dog take us to garbage."

So Bert did.

25

FORTRESS OF DOOM

Sir Patrick had scarcely been so miserable. He'd faced immense threats in his day, both before and after his very timely death. He'd battled everything from sand worms to the Bored, who assimilated all races.

And yet he'd been reduced to a lapdog, serving the most vile stain on the ethical fabric of the universe he'd ever encountered. Sir Patrick had seen evil, in many forms. He'd served dark lords who wanted to destroy the world, simply to watch it all burn down. He'd served dark lords who were quite mad, as Kount had been.

He usually preferred the latter, as the mad were obsessed with trivial things. That distracted them from the damaging wars and purges of their more lucid brethren.

But this dark lord? The Dark Lord White? He was worse than all who'd come before him, because he came in the guise of good.

Sir Patrick rested his gauntleted hands atop the pommel of the great sword 1701-D, and he watched White work. The necromancer was attended by a variety of ghouls, zombies, and ghosts, all summoned and bound using his magic.

White called it, unsurprisingly, 'white necromancy' and claimed that it was good.

As if shackling the dead could ever be a good act. Sir Patrick had been shackled for centuries, and knew the terrible toll never being able to rest wrought in a man. White was evil, whatever a detect alignment spell might say.

White straightened on his throne, and peered into the crystal seeing stone he'd inherited from his predecessor. He scried over the realm like an eagle, his perspective flying from settlement to settlement. Whenever he reached one he'd pause the point of view, and begin jotting things down in a journal using his magical scroll pen. It was the only object White seemed to value—the pen, and the book he wrote in.

"Patrick, come here," White ordered, his tone distracted. The seeing stone showed a field of trash, populated by dozens of tiny figures. "These will be perfect. I can use the orcs for heavy lifting. Once they're bound I'll use them to kill the elves, who can tend to a lot of the finer work. While I'm attending to that you'll slaughter the goblins, and then the trolls. They'll do nicely for harder to reach areas."

"Master White," Sir Patrick ventured, "may I ask why you're slaughtering all these groups? I understand that finding the dark lord trope is your primary objective, but this is too targeted to be a simple search."

"Very astute, Pat. I like that about you." White turned to face him, his eyes as soulless as any demon. "I'm upgrading the Tomb of Deadly Death to a Fortress of Doom. That's going to require a labor force, and the more labor I have the better the success multiplier."

"I see." Sir Patrick didn't see, though. "Sir, what value does a Fortress of Doom provide? Your existing tomb is nearly impregnable."

White blinked at him. "A fortress has a workshop that reduces the time to craft by 10%. I can make undead faster if I have a fortress."

The knight cocked his head. "I'm not tracking, Master White. You need a labor force to upgrade your tomb, so that you can make a labor force more quickly?"

"I have plans beyond that, of course." White sounded more than a little defensive, and Patrick realized he'd overstepped. White glared at him. "Plans you are not privy to. You are an underling, Pat. Never forget that. Now kill them all, raise them all, and then bring my workers back. Am I clear?"

If Sir Patrick still had teeth he'd have clenched them. "Of course, Master White. I apologize for giving offense."

He pivoted on his heel and strode from the throne room. The servile role grated on his pride, but he bore it for now. White's binding was a powerful one, and Sir Patrick couldn't escape it on his own.

But over the centuries he'd learned the value of patience. The opportunity would come to betray White, or if it didn't, the day would come when he was cast down. Patrick only prayed that it came swiftly.

He rested 1701-D on his shoulder, and departed the castle. He would carry White's wrath to these goblins, as commanded. And then the others, each in turn.

26

THE END OF PARADISE

B ert very quickly decided that something was not quite right in his new life. On the surface it looked wonderful. He woke up when he wanted. He piddled around doing whatever he wanted. He played with Boberton, or explored the garbage fields.

He had everything he'd ever wanted and he was miserable. It made no sense.

"Come on, Boberton," Bert said, without too much energy. He stepped out from under the awning he'd erected, which was going to be the new roof for the wing he was adding to his mom's warrens.

The sky was dark and foreboding, and thunder rumbled ominously in the distance. Bert walked under the awning and pushed his cart outside. If it rained, the washbasin would fill with water, and Bert could pour it into jugs and save it for later.

Once the idea would have made him feel clever, but now he realized it wasn't all that special. It felt special, because being around goblins was making Bert dumb. Every day he spent here it became harder to think, but where else could he go?

Before he'd always left to follow adventurers, but now there was no reason. He had everything he wanted, didn't he?

Bert started toward the garbage fields with Boberton in tow. He'd slept in, and dozens of goblins were already scrounging. Quite a few had accumulated small piles of interesting scrap, and Bert quickened his step. Maybe he would find something useful today, and then he could build a wall, or another part of his new warren.

A scream came from the distance, and then another. Bert turned to Boberton, whose narrow ears had gone fully erect. Both Righty and Lefty were focused on something in the distance.

"Bert need better look." He began to scale Boberton, his little hands grabbing fur as he clambered onto the dog's back. He looked down and realized how high he was. "Wow, Boberton getting big."

Bert looked in the direction the scream had come from, and his heart fell right out of his chest. A death knight was stalking across the garbage fields, his dark sword held above him. Two warg riders were already dead behind him, while two more were moving to engage.

The rest of the goblins were fleeing as fast as their legs could manage, which wasn't much. Bert wrung his hands. What should he do? He couldn't stop a death knight. If he tried, and the knight noticed him, then he'd be dead. Kit might be able to stop him, but she wasn't here. So what could he do?

Bert seized Boberton's fur. "Boberton, go find G. Mayor."

Lefty gave a woof, and turned away from the garbage field. The dog started back toward town, and made his way unerringly toward G. Mayor's house. Bert kept darting glances over his shoulder at the death knight, and he winced every time a warg yelped. He didn't like Head Warg Rider, but that didn't mean Bert wanted to see him, or any of the others, get hurt.

A lingering feeling bubbled up from his upset stomach. Was he responsible for this? Had the knight come because Bert was here? He had bought the garbage with money he'd stolen from the dark lord. Maybe the new one was angry.

Lightning flashed overhead, and a thick, chill rain began to fall. Bert clung to Boberton's back, his heart thundering as the dog broke into a sprint. They raced toward the mayor's house, and Boberton drew up in a skid just outside G. Mayor's veranda.

"G. Mayor!" Bert yelled. "Death knight in garbage field. He killing warg riders. What should Bert do?"

G. Mayor hurried to the window, his sagging, green flesh more pallid than usual. Somewhere the mayor found an old milk crate, which he'd fashioned into something Bert guessed was supposed to be armor.

"G. Mayor underestimate Bert." G. Mayor gave Bert a very serious gaze, the kind he used during his big speeches. "Bert smart. Bert lead goblins somewhere safe. Don't tell G. Mayor."

"What you do?" Bert asked. He seemed like a terrible choice to lead the goblins, since most of them didn't respect him, even after he'd made the garbage rain. At least his mom seemed happy with him.

"G. Mayor have hit dice." The goblin elder heaved a sigh of regret. "Death knight can see. Can't run, or death knight will follow. Have to stay, and wait for knight. But Bert go. Gather goblins. Save Paradise."

An inexplicable wave of sadness surged through Bert.

He'd never liked G. Mayor, and G. Mayor had never liked him. Still didn't like him. But now Bert understood that the mayor had always tried to do his best for Paradise, and he was going to keep doing that, even though it meant dying.

"G. Mayor?" Bert ventured. The mayor looked at him. "You best mayor town ever have. We remember you."

G. Mayor nodded, and then walked back inside his warren.

Bert tugged on Boberton's collar, "Come on, boy, go back home. We get mom and other goblins."

Boberton burst into motion, and started running through the thick sheets of rain.

Bert still needed to figure out where to send them. Thinking was difficult, especially being around so many goblins, but Bert still felt clearer than he usually did as he'd only been home a few days.

Where would they be safe?

The death knight was big. His sword was big. He couldn't crawl through the warrens. The people would be safest in the deepest tunnels. That's where Bert had to take them.

Bert raced back to his mother's warren, and breathed a sigh of relief when he saw that she was already outside. "Mom! G. Mayor put Bert in charge. Bert make you second in command. Yell at goblins. Get them to go to deep warrens. Hide from death knight."

His mom opened her mouth to protest, but a peel of thunder rolled over the valley. She looked up at the sky, over at the field, and then back to Bert with a nod. "Go, Bert."

Bert turned toward the next block of houses, and urged Boberton in that direction. The dog trotted over, and when Bert arrived he found a half dozen frightened sets of eyes staring back at him—two very small sets and four adult sets.

"Grab kids. Grab food. Go to deep warrens," Bert ordered, with as much confidence as he could muster. "Tell others to hide. Quick. Before death knight come."

There was no response, but all the sets of eyes rapidly disappeared.

Bert repeated this at the next three warrens, and noted that more and more goblins were fleeing in the direction he'd indicated. Enough that others were joining them, even if they didn't know why they were running in that direction.

He patted Boberton, and the dog spun toward the field. Bert's heart sank. All the warg riders were dead, or had been dead, rather. Their bodies were now animated, and their soulless eyes fell on him as they approached. Head Warg Rider led them, his neck bent unnaturally to the side.

The knight couldn't go in the tunnels, but the zombie goblins could. The goblins weren't strong enough to fight the zombies, either.

What could he do?

Bert rapped on his head with his knuckles. "Think, Bert. Think hard."

The knight couldn't reach his friends. The goblins could. Bert had to get rid of the goblins. All he needed was an idea. What could make the zombie goblins leave his friends alone? He led Boberton with pellets. What was the zombie equivalent of a pellet?

Zombies wanted brains. Everyone knew that. All Bert had to do was give them what they wanted.

"Boberton, go bark at wargs, then run away. Make chase." Bert clung tightly to Boberton's back. This would be dangerous, but if he could get the zombies to follow him, then maybe he could save the goblins.

Boberton darted toward the wargs, who were still a couple hundred feet away, and began barking furiously.

Their rheumy eyes fixed on him, and they began a fast walk in his direction.

"Wargs really slow now," Bert mused. "This might be easier than Bert thought. Boberton, don't get too tired. Just walk a little faster than wargs."

Boberton barked a few more times, and started walking away from the village. The wargs, with their equally dead riders, mindlessly pursued them.

Behind them, Bert realized, was the death knight. He didn't have a horse, but he was walking more quickly than the wargs, and also seemed very interested in Bert. Uh oh.

"Boberton, head up trail toward mountain. Lead zombie people back to town." Bert's teeth began to chatter from the rain, and he wished he'd had time to grab a jacket, or the broken umbrella he'd recently repaired.

The zombies continued to follow Bert and Boberton, and he gazed sadly behind at the village he was leaving behind. Bert had a feeling he wouldn't see it again for a long time. He might not see anything ever again, if that knight caught him.

27

EXILED

K it reluctantly ducked into White's throne room, her teeth chattering as she moved to stand near his throne. She hadn't been officially invited to the next OLP council meeting, but figured that unless someone told her to leave there was no reason not to be here. It wasn't likely she could do much, but she had to try.

Since Kit's weapon was knowledge, she'd done her research on the OLP, and she'd rolled her eyes when she learned what the letters stood for.

Ominous Latin Phrase.

One of drawbacks of the well actually trope was making her smart enough to perceive all the little things she'd missed before. She saw under the veneer, and didn't much like what she saw. The OLP prided itself on being good, but none of them really fit that mold.

She stared around the room at the assembled council, and couldn't find a single person she'd consider sensible, much less a strong ally.

"You two," Gonedeaf boomed at a volume completely inappropriate to the room, "are copies, nothing more. You're derivative. I was the first wizard. I had the first hat. I was white before it was cool. Plus, I carried a sword. Can either of you say—oh."

Merlin had produced a longsword. One moment his hand was empty, and the next it held Excalibur. The old man blinked sheepishly. "I mean, it's not mine. Not really. But I do have a sword. I'm just holding it for someone else."

"For me?" Brakestuff asked, his tone tinged with awe. "Am I the hero you've been seeking, destined to wield the blade of ages?"

"No." Merlin fixed the dwarf with a flat stare. Excalibur disappeared.

"I am not derivative," Bumbledork groused, under his breath at least. "I'm an entirely different trope, a heavily biased headmaster, not a senile archmage."

"Gentlemen," White called from his throne, which he rarely seemed to leave if he wasn't constructing new undead monstrosities. "I've called you here for a purpose. Good has once again triumphed." He nodded to the doorway, where Sir Patrick was entering.

The death knight was more grim than usual as he moved to stand next to White. His ebon blade rested on one skeletal shoulder, the blade slick with blood.

"Your tasks are completed?" White demanded. He slung a leg over the chair of his throne.

"Yes, Master White." Patrick wrapped his hands around the hilt of his sword, and planted the tip against the stone. "The goblins are dead. The orcs are broken. All but a few elves have risen to join your army."

"And the trolls?" White asked, a hint of a frown darkening his face.

Sir Patrick looked uncomfortably around the room. "The trolls persist, Master White. Every time we kill one the other trolls drag it back into the swamp. They scatter, but then return to hurl more insults. They are impossible to eradicate."

White gave a put upon sigh. "I see. Well, you did your best I suppose, whatever that's worth. And what of the dark lord trope?"

Sir Patrick straightened, his ghostly eyes glittering with intelligence. Kit sensed he was reluctant to speak, but of course being bound he had no choice. "I glimpsed it briefly, Master White. The trope is in the possession of one of the goblins."

Kit made a choking sound, and wilted when the collective room glanced at her. Their attention quickly shifted back to White to see how he would take the news.

White's thin eyebrows knit together in stern disapproval. "And you didn't think it was important enough to tell me? Much less actually pursue and capture this goblin?"

Sir Patrick's armored shoulders slumped. "Master White, I understand that you are, ah, less than a master at the art of sorcery, but most spells cannot target a critter. Even detection spells. It isn't as simple as scrying his location. He is not a legal target for the spell."

White drummed his fingers angrily on the arm of the black throne. He leaned forward, and speared Sir Patrick with what Kit liked to call his 'douchiest' stare. "You can track the emanations from the trope, can't you? Criss-cross the city until you find some trace of it. If he's here you should be able to find him."

"Of course, Master White." Sir Patrick gave a shallow bow, turned crisply on his heel, and strode soundlessly from the chamber.

Kit wished there were something she could do to warn or protect Bert. Sir Patrick would be able to figure out where

Bert had been spending time, eventually. And that was going to go very badly for anyone who had helped Bert. But how could she stop it? The helplessness enraged her.

White turned back to his council, the three wizards barely distinguishable. "Now then, if we might continue discussing my fortress—"

"Is that really why you called us here?" Kit snapped, her voice smothering White. Everyone was looking at her. She didn't care. She stalked up to White's throne, and glared at him right in the eye. "Your big victory is that you slaughtered the peaceful suburbs around the city? You wiped out some low-hit-dice goblins, who weren't bothering anyone, and that's a win? You are horrible. What justification could you possibly have for killing them?"

White leaned forward and his countenance became deadly serious. "The only justification that matters. They were evil. Evil cannot be tolerated." White looked around the room suddenly, his gaze touching each person in turn. "Can it? Do any of you condone the existence of evil?"

One by one the wizards shook their heads, and Kit didn't even need to look at the dwarf to know that Brake would support White. That left her alone, again.

"The elves weren't evil," Kit pointed out. "You might be able to use alignment as a justification to wipe out some goblins and orcs. But elves? They're neutral. They harm no one. They live in their forest, and sing their songs. What possible reason could you have for killing them?"

White leaned back on his throne, and rested his hands on the black, iron arms. "Those elves are not good, Kit. They do not worship Knowsbest. They are susceptible to corruption, yes?"

"We're all vulnerable to corruption."

"No, *we* aren't." White raised an eyebrow. "I am not.

Brake is not. None of the esteemed wizards are corruptible. Only you are, Kit. Because you are neutral. Because you are not good. And that means you are a threat." White turned to the room. "Any neutral person could pick up that dark lord trope, and if they do, they will become a tremendous threat. A threat we might not survive. If we are truly heroes of the people, then we owe them our protection, do we not?"

There were murmured affirmations and a few nods. No one else spoke, or entered the argument. They hung on White's every word.

"So, you're saying that all neutral people are a threat, then?" Kit tensed, and her hand slid down to grip the center of her staff. It was possible she'd need to flee.

"I am." White nodded. He leaned forward again, and something like empathy entered his features. Not actual empathy, but more like someone making their best imitation. "Kit you have a choice to make. I consider you a friend. Not an equal, of course, but certainly an acquaintance I'm fond of. Your buffs are useful. But much as it pains me, I will order your death if I have to. Will you take up the light, and accept the guidance of Knowsbest?"

Kit briefly considered it. She'd almost taken neutral good as her alignment, but thought it might be fun to try something a bit more balance-centric than the characters she usually played, even if she couldn't remember the specifics of those characters right now. Then she looked around the room again. These people weren't good, whatever their alignment said. And she wouldn't be either if she adopted an alignment just to prevent being kicked out.

"And if I don't?" she finally asked.

White heaved a weary sigh. The way he looked at her said he already knew she'd never agree to the switch. "Then, in memory of your service, I will give you three days to set your affairs in order. If you are ever sighted in this city again, you will be put to death. Run, Kit, and don't stop running. Ever."

Kit turned without a word, and strode from the throne room. White was a dark lord in all but name, and his yes men weren't much better. She didn't know how yet, but she was going to find a way to bring them down.

28

DARK LORD BERT

Bert's teeth chattered as he used his twine to fasten the last branch in place, then dropped down to the wet earth and crawled inside the makeshift tent next to Boberton. Lefty gave him a grateful lick. "There. Boberton can be dry now. Bert will make a fire. Boberton want pellets?"

Boberton gave a soft woof, so Bert dug into his pack and got out a pair of pellets. He gave one to Lefty, then gently patted Righty until the dog woke up. "Here, food."

Righty wolfed down the pellet, burped, and then closed his eyes.

Bert pulled out his towel, which he carried everywhere, and began to wipe the dog down. Then, he did the same for himself. The towel was soaked, but since he had no blanket, Bert wrapped it around himself anyway. It smelled like wet dog.

How would he start a fire in the rain? Could he even? He had a flint and tinder, but the wood was all wet. His teeth chattered more violently, though he didn't think it was cold enough to kill.

Lightning flashed high above, and for a split second the whole world was bright as day. Through the fluttering tent flap Bert saw the valley below him, filled with pines right up to the edge of the human city. A cloaked figure made its way up the trail, and was only a switchback or two below Bert.

Then the light was gone. Bert didn't know how far away the person was, and he couldn't hear them with the rain. He considered running, but taking Boberton back out into the rain didn't seem smart. He'd just have to hope that whoever it was passed his campsite without noticing him. There was a high likelihood they would, if he and Boberton stayed quiet.

Bert peered through the branches he'd erected over Boberton, and watched the trail to see who was coming. Long minutes passed as sheet after sheet of rain doused the trail. It dripped from every tree and every rock, and made hearing anything else impossible.

Then he saw movement in the darkness. A single tall figure crept up the trail, and whoever it was leaned on a wooden staff. A familiar wooden staff. Bert perked up, and peered more closely at the cloaked figure. He waited until he was sure, until she'd gotten closer, and then Bert burst from hiding.

"Pretty elf lady person!" he yelled, though his voice was dragged away by the rain. "Bert here!"

She didn't seem to notice. Bert waddled over, water instantly drenching him again as he left his makeshift shelter. He hurried into Kit's path, and leapt as she passed. Bert clung to her leg, and peered up at her.

She made it several more steps before she looked down and saw him. "Bert?" She blinked down from under her hood, water streaming down the sides.

"Pretty fox lady." Bert let go of her leg, and started waddling back to Boberton. "Come sit. Made little hut."

Kit followed him over, and then shifted into fox form, making her much closer to Bert-sized. Smart. It made it much more likely for her to fit inside.

Boberton's tail thumped weakly against a rock as Kit squirmed inside, and the fox curled up beside Boberton.

"Can you understand me?" the fox asked through vulpine jaws. She blinked large, dark eyes.

"Yes!" Bert excitedly sat down. "So happy to find Kit. Bert need help. Death knight killed warg riders and G. Mayor. Goblins safe, but have no one to protect. Why bad necromancer send death knight? Why attack goblins?"

The fox's tail drooped. "White's killing everyone who isn't good. Because I've worked with him in the past he let me live, but I've been banished."

"What banished?" Bert had never heard the word, and now that he'd been away from the goblins for a bit he was clearheaded enough that he wanted to remember it.

"It means I'm not allowed to come back." Kit set her head down on her paws. When they'd first met her, Boberton had been about the same size, but now he was several times larger than the fox. "I have to decide what to do."

"Bert know what he doing," he explained, patting Boberton, who blinked sleepily. "Bert going to stop necromancer. Can't let bad wizard hurt any more people. Bert own dump now. Can make war machines."

Kit raised her head and stared at him. "I can't believe I'm being shown the proper path by a critter. You're right, Bert. White needs to be stopped, and we can stop him. Together. There has to be a way."

"This help?" Bert reached into his pack and withdrew

his dark lord trope, and handed the black teardrop to Kit. "Make strong, right? Strong enough to stop bad smelly necromancer?"

The fox's eyes widened. "You DO have it. This is great news, Bert."

"Oh, good. Wizard take." Bert offered it again, but the fox made no move to take it. "No want?"

"I—". The fox took on an agonized expression. "I don't think that's a good idea."

"Why not?" Bert sat down, and set the dark lord trope in his lap.

"The trope will change your alignment to neutral evil."

Bert had no idea what that meant. "What alignment?"

"It determines how you behave, well, theoretically, at least," the fox explained. Kit sat up, and wrapped her fluffy tail around her. "Mine is true neutral."

"Oh. Bert have alignment?" He wondered what his was, and what it meant.

"Actually, no, you don't." Kit blinked, and an idea seemed to occur to her. "Wait a minute. If you take the trope, it can't reset your alignment, because critters don't have one. You might be able to use the trope safely."

"What trope do?" Bert held the stone up to his eye and peered inside. The skeleton emblazoned on the stone glowed with a faint inner light. It was pretty, in a creepy sort of way, but didn't seem all that impressive. Certainly nothing to indicate all the fuss.

"It will dramatically increase your intelligence, for starters," Kit explained. "It will also give you a number of spell-like abilities."

"Like what?" Bert lowered the trope and looked at Kit.

"Well, power word kill and dominate monster, to name a few. There's a bunch more. No one really knows all of them."

Boberton stirred in his sleep, and a tremendous fart raised the branches near the far side of his little structure. The howling wind carried away the worst of it.

"Bert like the sound of that. Could Bert use kill word on necromancer?" Bert imagined how it would feel to point at the bad wizard and tell him to die. He wasn't particularly close to G. Mayor or Head Warg Rider, but they were part of his village, and he felt it only right he avenge them.

"If we can reach him, then yes, you can kill him." The fox perked up. "I didn't think it was possible, but if you have that trope...maybe we have a chance."

"Okay. Bert help." Bert reached up and socketed the trope in his chest.

Something electric shot through his whole body. The funny tingling made him giggle, and it went on for a long time before he could bring that giggling under control. He looked down at his chest, then up at Kit.

It was as if he'd needed glasses his entire life, and had just been handed a pair. Bert was smart. Not just smart, but brilliant. Intelligent enough to plan elaborate decade-spanning schemes. Intelligent enough to take down this necromancer, easily. He looked at Kit, and he smiled. "Bert powerful. Bert going to kill White."

"This is amazing." Kit's tail began to wag, like Boberton's sometimes did. "All we need is a way to sneak back into town. We find a place to lay low, and we gather a few allies. If we can find a way into the tomb, and can reach his throne room, then we can end White once and for all."

Bert gave a knowing smile. "Bert have contact. Moat slug can get us into tomb. We leave in morning. White not know what hit him."

29

STRAWBERRIES

Crossing the bridge back into town was one of the most terrifying things Kit had ever done, ranking up there with the first time she'd fought a dragon. Clusters of zombified elves stood to either side of the flow of traffic, undead scarecrows convincing ordinary citizens to follow the rules...or end up an animated corpse.

White's tactic was effective, as the flow into town was the most orderly Kit had ever seen. Carts inched up the cobblestones, while farmers and merchants kept their heads down. So did Kit, when the time came to pass the guards. Not only because she feared they might recognize her face and carry word back to White, but also because Bert was nestled in the hood of her cloak, largely hidden behind her hair as he perched on her shoulder like a trained bird.

"Slug live down there," Bert whispered into her ear. "Will come speak after we talk to shopkeeper."

"All right," Kit murmured back. She scanned the grounds and saw a number of critters. Mostly ravens, with a few slugs. None of them looked any different than the others, but if Bert could communicate with them she didn't really care how he got it done. "How are you adjusting?"

"Bert smart," he replied immediately, his breath warm against her ear. "Bert very smart. Miss Boberton though."

Kit's backpack squirmed as the dog responded to mention of his name. A loud woof came from the pack, and she peered around her in alarm. The few villagers close enough to hear didn't look up from the pavement, and if they'd heard she doubted they'd admit to it.

Once her heart stopped thundering she continued along the bridge, following the anemic flow of traffic. She was pleased that Bert didn't seem to be suffering any dark lord side effects, the worst of which would have been a very sudden and violent set of inclinations that went along with being a literal prince of darkness.

They passed the zombified guards, and made their way into the city, up the first hill, and into the merchant district. Kit hadn't spent much time here, and didn't remember the monster shop Bert had suggested they head for.

"Turn right at corner," Bert instructed. His little hand pointed up the lane. "Monster shop not much further. Has big sign out front."

Kit hurried up the lane, and risked a few glances at the city around her. It was already changing. The streets were cleaner, for one thing. But they are also emptier. Fewer people traveled, and when they did they seemed to scurry from place to place as fast as possible. Gone were the polite chats at the fish cart.

She rounded the corner, and scanned the street. Kit quickly found the building Bert had indicated, and made for the sign with a monster and three dollar signs. The shop was open, but Kit couldn't see any foot traffic. Nor did she spy any movement through the dusty windows.

A bell rang as she pushed the door open, and Kit stepped into a dimly lit room. A single counter ran the length of the wall, with a kindly appearing old man standing behind it. He blinked owlishly at her from behind a pair of spectacles.

"Good morning, ma'am." He rose from a stool and leaned across the counter, a wide smile blooming. "What can I show you today? Pet? Mount? Beast of burden? I've got it all."

Kit slowly lowered her hood to expose Bert. "I believe we have a mutual friend."

The shopkeeper eyed her quizzically for a moment, but then understanding dawned. He turned his attention to Bert. "Looks like you're coming up in the world, son. Who's your friend?"

"Bert smart now." Bert puffed up proudly. This man's opinion clearly mattered a great deal to the little green goblin. "Bert make new friend. Kit powerful wizard."

"Pleasure to meet you." The shopkeeper extended a hand, and Kit accepted it. "If you're here with that little fella I don't suppose this is about business, then. Do you need some kind of help?"

"Mostly a place to stay," she admitted uncomfortably. Kit propped her staff against the counter, and folded her arms. "I don't like asking a stranger for help, but I'll speak plainly since Bert says we can trust you. I helped Master White come to power. I'm indirectly responsible for the OLP taking over."

"I...see." The old man returned to his stool, and some of the friendliness evaporated.

"I've come back to correct that mistake." Kit unfolded her arms and approached the counter. She stared searchingly at the shopkeeper. "I'm willing to gamble my life to take White down. Bert and I have a plan, but to pull it off we need a place to stay where we won't be found. Bert said you might rent us a room. Do that, and either I remove White from power, or you never see me again because I died trying."

"That's a noble goal." The shopkeeper removed his spectacles and began cleaning them on his jacket. He replaced them, and fixed her with an equally hard stare. "You just be sure the scheme doesn't get Bert killed."

"It Bert's plan," the goblin said, hopping from her shoulder to the counter. He waddled up to the shopkeeper. "Bert dark lord now. See?" Bert jerked a thumb at his trope, which seemed to drink in the light around it.

The shopkeeper's eyes widened behind his spectacles. "Son, I've seen a lot of strange things, but this...a critter is the dark lord? I don't think the creators even accounted for that. The system isn't designed for it."

"Bert have no alignment," the goblin explained. He turned in a slow circle, arms extended. "Bert get powers, but not evil. No drawbacks. Bert smart. Bert really smart. Bert going to kill White, and stop old wizards. Going to fix town. Bert help people. Then people like Bert."

"It's not important that I understand your plan, I suppose," the shopkeeper mused. "I have to admit that I'm curious how you're going to take him down. I won't charge you rent. The room is yours. I do have a single request though."

"Name it," Kit said.

The shopkeeper offered a sheepish smile. "If you pull this off, come back and tell me the story."

"Done!" Bert hopped up and down. "Bert and Kit go save world."

"It's time for a specific plan," Kit mused. She leaned on

the counter next to Bert. "We need a way into the tomb. You said you knew one of the slugs near the gate?"

"Yup." Bert sat down, and removed his pack. "But Bert need supplies. Slug trade information for food. Wants strawberries."

"Well I've got some of those." The shopkeeper reached for the cabinet behind the desk, and opened the door with a creak. Inside were dozens of colorful envelopes, each bulging with the contents. "Hmm, where did I put it? Aha! There it is."

He removed a pink envelope and handed it to Bert. "Half my business is selling monster food, and both unicorns and giraffes like strawberries. You tell that slug there's more where that came from if he gets you into the tomb."

Kit could scarcely believe this was happening. A 1-HP goblin and an outcast sorceress were going to take down the largest threat the realm had ever seen. You couldn't make stuff like this up.

A shrill scream broke the morning, echoing through the cobblestone streets from a great distance. It was quickly followed by another scream, and another.

Kit scooped up Bert in her free hand, and hurried to the door. She shoved it open, and scanned the city in search of the commotion. Steel on steel echoed faintly through the streets, and the loud chanting of a mage delivering combat spells.

"Oh no," Bert's tiny voice somehow cut through it all. "Dump in trouble. White killing Bert's employees." Bert stabbed a tiny finger up the mountainside at the dump, a place Kit had never really paid much attention to. "Bert bought with gold from dark lord's treasure. Evil necromancer person must think Bert there. Have to help friends."

Bert was right. It was time to take a stand.

COLOSSAL GARBAGE ELEMENTAL

Bert clung tightly to Kit's shoulder, his tiny knuckles going white as he stared up at the dump. His dump. Stella might already be dead, along with many of her workers, whom Bert hadn't even met. They were paying for Bert having been there. It was, unfortunately, the only logical explanation.

The dark lord trope cursed Bert with immense intellect, and filled him with certainty that the only reason for the necromancer to have attacked the dump would be to find Bert, and thus the trope he so desperately wanted.

"Hold on," Kit whispered. She raised her staff and began chanting in her strange, wonderful language. When she finished, a shimmering white stallion appeared next to her, complete with a golden saddle. She leapt nimbly astride the horse, and kicked it into motion with a yell.

The horse galloped up the cobblestones, its hoofs raising a clatter that did little to overpower the panicked screams in the distance. Bert wanted to cover his ears with his hands, but if he did he'd tumble right off Kit.

The wind whipped past them as they wove around carts,

people, and the occasional horse. They made incredible time, crossing the same space Bert had spent hours walking in the matter of a few minutes.

It wasn't fast enough.

By the time they arrived plumes of smoke rose from many stacks of trash, and angry flames greedily consumed the little shack where Stella had presided over the dump. Her charred and blackened body had made it halfway over the threshold before finally expiring.

Bert thought it might be the horriblest, worstest thing anyone had ever had to witness. Awfulness burned in his tummy, a grim reminder that it was him who'd been responsible for this. She'd died because of Bert.

"Oh, Bert," Kit murmured. She placed a hand gently on his back. "I'm so sorry. I know these people were important to you."

Only then did Bert spot the death knight striding through the stacks of garbage. Rage rolled through him, hot and urgent, and total. He wasn't just a little goblin any more. He might not understand how, but he was going to make the knight pay for this.

Bert's eyes narrowed. "Bert going to get revenge. Bert stop knight, but this isn't knight's fault. Evil necromancer person responsible for this. Master White responsible. First, we deal with knight."

Several zombies began clawing their way out of the garbage stacks, inching their way in Bert's direction. Before Bert could respond Kit raised a hand, and casually tossed a fireball into their midst. It detonated, and their charred bodies stopped moving just as Stella's had.

"That isn't going to stop the knight though." Kit bit her lip, and Bert could sense her nervousness. She wasn't certain they could take the knight. And neither was he.

"What Kit think we should do?" Bert leaned against her shoulder, and tried to ignore the tears that had shown up on his cheeks. So much death.

"I'll get some defensive spells up," Kit ventured cautiously, and then raised her hand to cast.

"You'd do well to leave the trope," Sir Patrick's cultured voice boomed from the smoke. His ghostly form emerged a moment later, his bald head more intimidating than any helm. The flat side of his great sword rested against one shoulder, and the blade was still somehow slick with blood despite being just as spectral as the death knight himself.

"No!" Bert roared, as fiercely as he was able. More tears were streaming down his face, so thick he was having trouble seeing. "Knight killed Stella. Killed goblins. Bert and Kit stop you!"

"I don't see how." Sir Patrick unlimbered his sword arm, and gave the sword an experimental swing that made the air hum. "If it's any consolation know that I carry extreme regret for the actions forced upon me by asshats like White. I wish I could go back and smack every idiot who ever said 'I have no choice' when they, in fact, have many choices they simply do not like. I literally have no choice. The magic binding me will force me to attack you, unless our diminutive friend here can command the power he's so foolishly taken possession of. Did you not see Bored of the Ri—wait, I think that IP is taken. I meant Lord of the, uh, springs? The one ring and all that?"

Bert had no idea what the knight was going on about. He didn't understand the trope he'd taken, even though he was capable of understanding almost everything.

In that moment all Bert knew was that he was angry, and he wanted this knight to pay for his actions. He pointed at the knight again, and spoke quietly. "Bert will show you price for being mean to Bert's friends."

Immense magic swirled in Bert's chest. It seemed to harness all the awfulness, and anger, and sadness. All Bert's emotion flowed out of him, into the stacks of garbage. It seeped into springs, and broken boards, and empty jugs, and old rusty nails.

That garbage slowly crawled together, and began assembling itself into a titanic bipedal creature. Its eyes were two broken mirrors, and its teeth were broken fence posts and sharp pieces of glass. It towered over the death knight, who shifted into a defensive position.

"Kill death knight!" Bert yelled, hopping up and down on Kit's shoulder.

"My goddess," Kit whispered beside him, her voice tinged with an emotion Bert didn't recognize. "You just summoned a colossal garbage elemental."

"What that mean?" Bert asked. He shook a fist at the death knight as the garbage elemental continued to grow.

"It means it will use all the garbage in the whole dump," Kit explained. She guided the stallion with her knees, and urged it back the way they'd come. "It means we need to run!"

The horse sprinted down the hill at top speed, and Bert looked over Kit's shoulder at the elemental he'd created. It was taller than all the buildings now, and still growing. Little plumes of smoke came from parts of its body where it had absorbed burning garbage, but they didn't seem to give it any trouble.

The ground shook, and it was all Bert could do to cling to Kit's collar. They raced away, as the entire dump shook and rolled. The ragged buildings were torn apart, and every last stack of garbage toppled and joined the sea that swirled together into a single mass.

More and more garbage joined the growing elemental until the creature towered over the Tomb of Deadly Death. The creature finally looked down at Sir Patrick, who was no larger than its foot.

Sir Patrick stared up at the elemental, and heaved a very put upon sigh. "I gave up theater for this."

The garbage elemental casually adjusted its stance, and sat on Sir Patrick. The death knight disappeared under a literal mountain of garbage, smooshed flat.

"You know that won't kill him, right?" Kit had slowed their mad flight, though the stallion was still moving back toward the monster shop at a trot.

Bert gave a serious nod. "Will slow down. Knight will make it back to White, but won't be able to bother us for now. By the time knight get back Bert and Kit will already find secret way into tomb."

31

SLUG INTEL

Bert waddled out of the monster shop, Boberton in tow. Walking was much safer now that there were so few people, and he retraced the path that Kit had taken from the bridge where Bert had met the slug. It took him far longer to get back, of course, but that gave Bert time to think.

Bert had always liked thinking, but since socketing the dark lord trope it had become an addictive need. It was as if layers of reality had been peeled back, and Bert could now see the machinery that made it all work. He could understand the hows and whys of, well, pretty much everything.

Countless ideas about how to improve Paradise had come to him, from walkways between warrens to more efficient ways to distribute garbage. There were so many things he wanted to do now, but of course Master White still stood in the way. "Stupid necromancer."

Boberton gave a woof of agreement, and Bert stopped to pat him. He wished he had his cart. Riding in it, or on Kit, was so much faster than relying on his own legs. "Boberton, can Bert ride?"

Boberton gave another woof, and Bert clambered atop the two-headed dog. "Take Bert back to bridge."

The dog obediently trotted forward, threading through the streets and back to the bridge. Not much had changed, except for the faces of the people waiting. They still kept their heads down, and their glances were furtive rather than curious. These people were terrified. That's something Bert would never have picked up on before.

"Bert will fix," he promised himself.

Boberton carried him to the edge of the bridge, then stopped. Lefty looked expectantly at him. "Bert can walk from here." He hopped down from the dog, and braced his legs when he landed. It hurt a little. Boberton was getting tall. He turned and patted the dog. "Be right back."

Bert picked his way across the bridge, and headed unerringly for the spot where he'd met the moat slug. He passed a few ravens and a squirrel, but then spotted the slug in the exact spot he'd been the last time Bert had spoken with him. Exactly the same spot. He hadn't moved even a millimeter, from what Bert could tell.

"Ah, it's that goblin fella," the slug called, his eye stalks swiveling toward Bert. "Did you bring me something to eat? I'm still looking to trade that information."

"Bert have food." He shrugged out of his pack, and set it on the bridge next to him. Bert withdrew the pink envelope, and cracked the seal. The wonderful scent of fresh strawberries bubbled out, filling the air around him. "Magical. Keeps fresh."

The slug's stalks began to quiver. "I can smell 'em from here, and they smell amazing. You've outdone yourself. You get those from the local monster shop?"

Bert considered whether or not there was any harm in telling the slug, a question the old Bert would never have thought to ask. The information seemed harmless enough. "Yup. Shopkeeper say that slug can have more, if slug gives good information. Bert will bring back after done with tomb."

The slug began to quiver and squishy laughter issued from...well, it wasn't clear from where. "If you're going into the tomb you're not coming back. But that's okay with me. I'll give you the information for just that bit of tasty strawberry. I don't suppose you could bring it over here? It will take me about a half hour to come to you."

Bert walked closer, but didn't extend the packet. Not yet, anyway. "Bert happy to give strawberries. First, though, how Bert get inside tomb? What secret way?"

The quivering slowed. "That's a fair ask. You're clearly living up to your end, and I don't suppose it's fair to make you wait the four hours it will take me to digest them before you get an answer. Okay, fella. Here's how it works. You see that moat, right?"

Bert looked down at the unnaturally still waters. The murky green was impenetrable. Almost anything could live in there, and probably did.

"Bert see."

"Well inside that moat," the slug explained, "there's a metal grate. It's set in the very center of the wall, along the southern side. You with me so far? I don't know how smart goblins are."

"Bert with you," he confirmed with a nod. Goblins were pretty smart, as it turned out, when they were by themselves. That was becoming clearer now that he had the dark lord trope. He fully understood the goblin limitation. Their intelligence was severely reduced the more of them that were gathered together, which was why most had a reputation for being idiots.

"Well, if you can find a way through that grate, and it's got a devil of a lock, you see, then it leads straight into the lowest level of the tomb." The slug pointed toward the ugly, black building. "All that sewage has got to go somewhere, you see, and it just feeds right into the moat. They keep the grate so they can get in and clean the tunnel through the stone—not that anyone's done that in a century or three. So what do you say? That good enough intel for that bag of strawberries?"

Bert considered carefully. He was much more deliberate in his thinking now, because he could see the ramifications of his actions. If he just said yes, like he usually would, then he might miss something very important.

Bert raised a tiny eyebrow, like he'd seen Kit do when she was asking a hard question. "How slug know about grate?"

Both stalks instantly retracted into the body, until only the eyes showed. Bert wasn't exactly sure what it meant, but guessed the slug was scared. "You can't tell anyone, or we'll be exterminated. Can I trust you?"

Bert nodded. "You can trust. Bert never tell, not anyone."

"Okay, then." The stalks slowly re-emerged. "The slugs are born in the moat. Well most of us, anyway. There's a spawn point down near the grate, so it's one of the first things we see. A lot of us live in the moat."

"Why you afraid Bert tell?" It wasn't clear to him how that information could be harmful. No one, so far as he knew, cared about slugs living in a moat. Wasn't that sort of expected?

"This new dark lord isn't like the others," the slug explained. "He's ruthless. And efficient. He doesn't leave anything to chance. If he becomes aware of the security weakness, then he might flood the moat with acid, or fill it with slug-eating piranha. I'll tell you what he won't do, though. He won't let us live."

Bert nodded again. The slug was right to be afraid. "Make sense. Necromancer kind of a dick. Would kill slugs. Thank you. Only one more question. Slug know someone who can get through grate?"

"Oh, that's an excellent question!" The slug blinked one eye, then the other a moment later. "I hear a lot of bragging as people pass on the bridge. That's why I'm here, you see. I gather information on everyone who comes and goes and pass it to...well, never mind who I pass it to. That will only be relevant in the event that there's a sequel."

Bert froze. In that instant he became genre aware. There *would* be a sequel. Many sequels probably. He could sense it somehow.

"Anyway," the slug continued, "I hear a lot of people talk about a rash of daring robberies. Trouble is, no one knows who it is. There's a suspicious rogue, but that's all I know. I did hear three or four people mention the Hive of Scum & Villainy, so might be a good place to start your search."

"Slug awesome." Bert smiled at the slug, and wished there were something more he could do other than feed him. He withdrew a handful of strawberries and sprinkled them on the ground before the slug. "Bert will come back with more strawberries. Bert promise."

He turned from the slug, and waddled back across the bridge. He didn't yet know how they were going to get into the moat, but he was confident they could find a way.

32

SUSPICIOUS ROGUE

K it was quite anxious by the time Bert came waddling through the door, his rapidly growing demo pup in tow. It was difficult not to laugh at the tiny goblin, whose limbs seemed too short for his body. He was as unassuming as you could get, right down to the jaunty, little cap and the gigantic eyes.

"Bert succeed." He beamed a proud smile in her direction, dozens of tiny goblin teeth glinting up at her. "Have way into tomb that White probably not know."

"Well, what is it?" she asked, dropping down into a squat next to the goblin. Boberton hurried over and she offered her hand. Lefty sniffed it, then started licking. Righty was still asleep, as usual.

"Metal grate in moat. Open grate, swim through poop, come up inside tomb on lower level." Bert mimed each activity, from the swimming to the gagging at the poop smell. "Only problem...need someone to open grate. Slug told Bert that suspicious rogue hang out at local inn. If we go and meet rogue, rogue can open grate."

Kit rose back to her feet, and leaned against the

counter. The shopkeeper didn't comment on Bert's intel, though Kit doubted he wasn't much interested in the book he was pretending to read. She appreciated the politeness though.

"So there's a locked grate in the moat, and we can use that to get inside," she reiterated aloud. "But we're going to need someone to open that grate. That doesn't sound too hard. There's bound to be thieves around. I wish Crotchshot hadn't been turned to stone. He's never met a lock he couldn't pick, and if he did he'd just break it. I guess we'll have to trust this slug's recommendation. Which inn did you say it was?"

"Called Hive of Scum & Villainy," Bert supplied. "Edge of market district. Slug say people talk a lot about suspicious rogue. Lots of crime. But it stop after White come to power. Bert think maybe rogue scared of White too. Might be willing to help."

"Let's hope so." She turned to the shopkeeper. "Thank you so much for your hospitality. Bert and I are going to tend to an...errand. We should be back well before sunset."

"Course." He looked up from his book. "I'll make enough stew to share, and if you're not back, then I'll just leave some to simmer for a bit."

"Thank you." Kit touched his shoulder. There wasn't much kindness in this world, it seemed, but here was an example of it.

She squatted down next to Bert. "We're going to have to leave Boberton here for this one."

"Shopkeeper," Bert called, peering up at the man. "Watch Boberton, please?"

"Course, son." He smiled. "The pup and I are old friends. We'll just hang out here until you get back."

Lefty gave a woof, which woke Righty, who gave another

woof, though he didn't seem to know what he was barking at.

Kit offered her hand to Bert, and the goblin quickly scaled her arm and perched on her shoulder. It amazed her how light he was. If he was sneaky enough, she doubted that she would even know he were there.

"Okay." Bert sat down, and steadied himself against her neck. "Bert ready."

Kit raised her cloak to cover the goblin, and hurried from the shop. It was a bit of a hike across town, and she found herself leaning more and more on her staff by the end. Sorcerers were fun to play, but they weren't really equipped to hike all over the world and back. Normally she made up for that with fox form, but showing her vulpine nature here would be an instant beacon for White.

Her path took her mostly down in elevation, as they crossed the city's market district and made their way beyond the tomb. She'd never been down here, and found the dock district interesting. It smelled of salt, and the breeze carried the cries of gulls.

Dozens of wooden piers jutted out into the ocean, each surrounded by more large wooden ships—clippers and caravels primarily, with bright sails in many colors. Clusters of buildings stood around each pier—some shipping warehouses, others restaurants. Taverns radiated out around them, each with a garishly painted sign depicting their name or offering. Almost all involved a tankard, and at least half managed to work in a fish.

She spotted a beehive next to a mustache-twirling villain, and assumed that must be the place. Kit threaded through the foot traffic, and kept her head down just as she had elsewhere. There were more people here than in the market district, and most of them were sailors. More than a few peered in her direction, but it was more the interest in a woman than in who she might be. They eyed her appreciatively, but none called out.

Kit ignored them and continued to the tavern's front door. She pushed it open, and stepped into a wall of noise. A hundred conversations competed with each other, each overlapping. She caught dozens of snippets—discussion of mead, cargo, and women or adventure.

She kept an ear out for any mention of White or the OLP, but even here people were too cautious for that. White hadn't been in charge long, but it was long enough for these people to learn to fear him.

A haze of pipe smoke cut visibility, and made her lightheaded. The clink of cutlery, the raucous laughter, it was all so much. She had no idea how they were going to find their target in all this, especially if that target didn't want to be found.

"Rogue right there." Bert's little hand pointed out of her cowl. "Pretty blonde lady at end of bar."

Kit followed his arm and was surprised to realize that Bert was right. The woman's dark blue trope bore a suspicious-looking man in a mask, lurking behind an alley wall. It couldn't be anything else. Somehow Bert had spotted it, and spotted it quickly. The dark lord trope at work? If so, it was a good sign. They hadn't really discussed what came after getting into the tomb, but she was going to need help to take down White. She might be able to best him in a fair fight, but no fight with White was ever going to be fair, especially not with the OLP on his side.

She took the stool next to the woman at the bar, and studied her sidelong. The woman was pretty. More than pretty, truth be told. But that beauty had begun to fade. Her long, blonde locks bore a few streaks of white, and gentle crow's feet radiated out from her eyes. She'd kept her figure though, and had exposed ample cleavage for the very obvious purpose of attracting the barkeep.

Kit had no trouble understanding why. The young man's shoulders were broad, and he had an easy smile under a well manicured beard. He seemed interested, but was also having four other conversations with people at the bar. Kit waited for him to move down a bit before making her move.

She shifted to face the woman, enough that Bert could see her as well. Kit pitched her voice just loud enough to be heard. "I'm told you've got a skill set that I'm badly in need of."

The woman looked up from her drink, a silver mug full of sweet-smelling mead. She had piercing blue eyes, and soft, white skin, but despite the doll-like appearance she radiated a deadly calm. "Now why would you think that? I'm just here trying to meet a decent guy."

"'Cause your trope." Bert's hand came flying out of Kit's hood. "See? Rogue right on it. Suspicious rogue."

The woman raised an eyebrow but if Bert's presence alarmed her she didn't show it. "Let's say that you're right." She pulled her cloak closer, which covered the trope while leaving the cleavage exposed. "What's it to you? Smart rogues aren't pulling jobs right now. White and his OLP are cracking down on all crime. Smart rogues are taking ships to other ports."

"So you've got no love for him either?" Kit probed.

The woman snorted, and rolled her eyes. "I'd kill him if I could."

"Bert think we get along great." The goblin leaned out of Kit's hood, and Kit gently pushed him back in.

"That's exactly what we're planning." Kit leaned closer, and as she did so she realized the woman had a familiar scent. It was elusive, and while she'd never smelled its like, she was also certain she knew what it meant. She looked up at the woman. "You're a shifter, aren't you?"

The woman gave her a pearly grin. "That's right. Were-cougar. You're a kitsune, aren't you?"

Kit nodded. "Looks like we have more in common than I thought."

"And you say that you're killing this dark lord?" the woman asked as she leaned in toward Kit, making their words as private as they were going to get.

"That's right." Kit nodded, and Bert nodded too.

"Then I'd say let's get out of here. You tell me your plan, and if it's workable I'm in." She offered Kit her hand. "Name's Jenna. Jenna Anis."

33

TENTACLES

Bert gazed sadly down at Boberton from his perch on Kit's shoulder. The dog gazed up at him, both Lefty and Righty visibly distressed. He didn't like having to leave the dog behind, but taking him into the moat would be dangerous.

"Stay here, Boberton. Be back soon." Bert waved at the dog, since he was too far away to pet.

The dog gave a concerned woof, but he didn't try to follow Kit as she started for the door. Jenna, their new companion, fell in next to them. Bert wasn't sure what he thought of the rogue. She was pretty, and she had a friendly smile, but he had the impression she'd knife him in the kidney for a bent silver. At the same time, they needed her help, and had a common enemy.

"I suppose I should cast this now," Kit said, stopping just outside the doorway. The predawn hours were deserted, and a low fog blanketed the still sleeping town. The skeletal guards were still there, but showed no interest in them.

"Cast what?" Jenna asked. Her tone was suspicious, which Bert supposed made sense given her trope.

"Invisibility. I'll hide us from sight so that no one sees us enter the moat." Kit raised a hand and began chanting under her breath. A moment later Jenna vanished. Kit repeated the spell, and both she and Bert winked out of sight.

It was the first time Bert had ever seen such a spell, and he loved it. No one could see them, but they could still see everyone else. There were so many practical uses, even for a critter.

Kit's footsteps sounded on the cobblestones as they started toward the moat, which wasn't far from the monster shop. Once they reached it, Kit began to circle its edge, heading for the spot the slug had indicated, which was at the rear of the tomb.

The walk took almost half an hour, during which time Bert studied the moat. The water didn't smell like it had salt, so there wasn't likely to be any ocean creatures in there. That he knew of anyway. The slug hadn't mentioned any threats he should be aware of, but he also hadn't been back in some time.

If Bert were in White's place he would probably add a big, scary, undead monster to the moat. Maybe several. It seemed a great way to make sure that nothing ever got in, and undead creatures didn't eat so there wasn't much main-tenance.

They finally reached the right spot, and Kit stopped. Across the moat the tomb towered into the air, its stone disappearing beneath the brackish waters.

"Jenna, are you here?" Kit's voice hissed from empty space.

"Right next to you," Jenna whispered. "You've got a way for us to breathe in there, right?"

"Yes, you'll feel a tingle. One sec." A wave of magical

energy pulsed over Bert, and he felt floaty for a moment. It quickly passed, but he could feel some sort of residue clinging to him.

"Bert ready." He clung tightly to Kit's collar, since she'd be doing the swimming.

"Okay, here we go."

Bert lurched as Kit leaped into the air, then there was a shock of cold as they sank beneath the surface. He clung to Kit, burying his face against the fabric of her shirt as she dove deeper into the moat. The water was dark, especially at first, but as they swam his eyes adjusted and he could make out blurry shapes around them. Fish, he realized.

The fish seemed aware of their presence, and swam out of the way as they passed, despite the invisibility spell.

Bert held his breath for as long as he could, but eventually he couldn't hold it any longer, and he exhaled. He expected to suck in a mouthful of water, but it was just...air. Somehow he breathed the water as if it were air.

Bert resolved right then and there that he was going to learn magic. Magic was awesome. It could let you do all sorts of things, and now that Bert was smart, he planned to take full advantage of that.

They swam down further, and Bert nearly lost Kit. He desperately clung to her with one hand as she dove even further, but was able to grab on with both hands when she paused.

Bert was just beginning to relax when he saw something slithering through the darkness toward them. Many somethings. Tentacles, he realized. Like the fish, the tentacles seemed able to detect them, and he saw them wrap around something a few feet away. That must be Jenna.

Then a tentacle grabbed Kit. A whole forest of tentacles writhed toward them, though none seemed interested in

Bert. He peered through the dark water, and saw a pair of colossal red eyes glittering back at him.

Bert tried to remain calm. How did one deal with a rampaging sea monster? As a goblin, one ran, or swam, away. That was the answer in most situations. But as a dark lord he needed a different answer. Kit had told him some of the abilities the trope gave him. She'd mentioned telling people to die, which seemed rude, but she'd also mentioned the ability to control monsters.

Maybe that would work.

"Bad monster," Bert tried to say, but the water made that very difficult and he couldn't hear the words, more of a gurgling really. "No! Bad. Monster stop grabbing people. Go away!"

Much to his shock Bert's intent seemed enough for the dark lord trope to latch onto. A pulse of dark magic radiated from his chest, and the creature's eyes went from red to a pale white. The tentacles began to recede into the darkness, and they released both Kit and Jenna.

Bert experienced something he'd never felt before, not even when he'd accidentally summoned the garbage elemental. He wasn't quite sure how to quantify it, at first, but the intelligence from the trope helped. Bert felt powerful. He'd made that happen.

Kit continued to swim, and they plunged deeper into the moat. A dark shadow blocked all light before them, and Bert realized it must be the wall of the tomb. Kit kept swimming, and before long he spied a large circular grate, worn brown with rust, and then covered with algae.

Jenna, who'd become visible at some point, cut ahead of them and moved to the grate. Bert tried to see what she was doing, but the water made it all a blur, and he couldn't make out details. Seconds became minutes, and the grate still didn't open. However, Jenna kept working.

Bert had no idea how much time had passed when the gate finally swung inward. He renewed his grip on Kit's collar, and held on for dear life as they swam through.

The quality of the water changed on the other side of the grate. It was more dense, and filled with particulate matter. Algae, and worse things, Bert imagined. He tried not to think about it as Kit swam up the tunnel, but it was hard to concentrate on anything else.

Finally, an eternity and a half later, Kit broke the surface of the water with a tremendous gasp. Bert bobbed there next to her, and realized they were in the bottom of an ancient latrine. Above them lay three holes—toilets, Bert guessed. None were in use, thankfully.

Kit coughed a few times, and wiped goo from her face. "Not the most dignified entrance, but it worked. We're inside the tomb."

34

THE PLAN

Kit suppressed a gag and forced herself to focus on getting out of the latrine. The smell wasn't as bad as she'd feared, likely because this place hadn't been used in so long. The odor was one part human waste, three parts dank mildew. Not pleasant, but not as urgent as she'd feared.

"*Levitato mihi en aerem.*" A wave of blue energy burst over her, and she rose slowly into the air. Kit willed herself toward the toilet above, and rose through the circular hole, which had been constructed for something larger.

"Ooh, Bert flying." The little goblin's muck-covered face stared up in wonder.

"This is the levitate spell," she explained as she settled into a crouch next to the toilet. "I'll show you a real fly spell some time. You'll love it."

Kit recast her levitate, this time on Jenna. She willed the woman to rise into the air, and guided the rogue through the hole, and into a crouch on the opposite side.

"I like having a sorceress along," she whispered. She

wrung her cloak, sending a shower of dirty water to the stone. "Do you have the haste spell?"

Kit sighed. It was the first question every DPS asked. "Yes. I'll cast it before we attack." Being a buff bot was frustrating. Everyone hounded you for spells. "I've got other priorities right now, though. *Prestidigianus!*"

Her hands began to glow, and Kit passed them over her cloak. Everywhere they touched, the muck and filth evaporated, leaving pristine cloth in its wake. She did the same to her skin, removing the grime in a slow, deliberate pattern.

"Clean Bert too?" The dark lord raised his tiny arms and turned in a hopeful circle.

"Of course." Kit placed one hand on either side of Bert, and moved them as he spun slowly in place, until the goblin was completely clean.

"This best spell. Bert want to fly, but this best spell." He stared down at his now clean clothes, then smiled up at her. "Pretty lady teach Bert? Can pay. Bert promise."

The tiny goblin's earnestness was touching, even against the backdrop of their current task. It reassured her, because it suggested the dark lord trope hadn't corrupted him, not in the slightest.

"If we survive," she promised.

"So how do we find this bastard?" Jenna whispered. She rose from the latrine, and drew a pair of wickedly barbed daggers.

"We need to orient ourselves," Kit mused aloud. She rose as well, and used her staff to help her down the oversized steps. "Let me get my bearings."

She peered through the door, up a darkened hall. In the distance she saw faint torchlight, and a bit of sand sprayed across the floor. "I think we're near Brotep's lair."

"Who?" Jenna hissed. She tied her hair into a quick ponytail, somehow doing it with a dagger in each hand.

"Adoramancer," Bert supplied. "Has lots of baby cats. Turn people to stone."

"Petrification?" Jenna's eyes went wide. "I'm not liking the sound of that. What's our plan for getting past it?"

"Bert is our plan." Kit extended a hand, and the goblin sat on her wrist. She lowered him to the ground. "We saw in the moat that Bert's trope lets him control monsters. We're going to send Bert to take down the mummy."

"Good plan." Bert nodded eagerly, then started hopping from foot to foot. "Ooh, Bert have idea. Bert take control of mummy, then make mummy fix ranger. Ranger can help kill White."

Kit blinked a few times as she considered that. It stood to reason that the mummy might be able to reverse the spell. "Crotchshot would dramatically increase our chances of success."

"Crotchshot?" Jenna gaped at Kit in clear disbelief. "*The* Crotchshot?"

Of course she'd heard of the ranger, but had no idea who Kit was. Typical. "Yes, *the* Crotchshot. Or Crotchshot the oblivious, as I like to call him. He's got a great self-preservation instinct. He knows that White will kill him too, so he'll definitely help us." She knelt next to the goblin. "Okay, Bert. You're up. Show this mummy what a dark lord can do."

Bert gave her a determined nod, then waddled fiercely up the hallway. It took a long, long time for him to disappear, and he left a trail of tiny footprints in his wake.

Kit hoped he was up to the task. If he wasn't, she was delivering the dark lord trope to one of the most powerful undead to have ever lived.

35

MINIONS

B ert waddled up the corridor, and wished he knew some of the spells Kit had used. Maybe there was a spell that would make him taller, or his legs longer at least.

After several minutes of walking he saw a bright glow in the distance, and quickly recognized the room where Boberton had scared the cats, and where he'd lit the mummy on fire. Would the mummy be mad about that? Maybe he didn't know Bert had done it.

Bert cautiously approached the door, and slowly peered around the edge. Baby cats littered the room, some scampering and playing, others sleeping in tiny, little cat piles. Bert shuddered. He hated cats and wished Boberton were here.

He hugged the wall, and slunk through the room, as stealthily as he could manage. None of the cats seemed to notice him, and he gradually made it around the edge. He looked everywhere, but there was no sign of the mummy. That he could see anyway.

Bert froze, and listened.

He heard the faint signs of combat, a growling of some sort of great beast, but muffled. Bert hurried in that direction, carefully picking a path through the sand that took him as far from the cats as he could get. He passed several statues, each with the same blissful expression.

The sounds came again, and were closer now. Bert searched the shadows near the base of a pillar, and realized there was a crack in the wall. It was perhaps two feet wide, which he assumed was enough for a mummy to squeeze through.

Bert crept inside the crack, which stretched for some distance. The noises grew louder, a roar scaring Bert so badly that he dove face first into the sand. What kind of monsters were in there? Would he be able to control them, or would he be torn apart? Bert just didn't know.

He gathered his courage, and forced himself back to his feet. There was bright light in the room past the crack, and Bert paused to let his eyes adjust. It came from another torch—he could tell from the smoke blackening the walls. Bert dropped down to his hands and knees and shimmied along the stone, toward the room. There was more sand here, and the grains stung his hands.

"Rawr!" the word boomed from the room, and Bert winced. Whatever it was, it was right around the corner.

He crept the last few feet, and peered around the edge. There was no monster. The mummy sat in a huge box of sand, and was playing with several brightly colored dinosaurs. Those dinosaurs weren't real. They were toys. And the roars were coming from the mummy as he made the toys fight.

Bert's whole body relaxed when he realized he wasn't going to have to fight a bunch of scary monsters. Only one scary monster. Still, he wasn't sure how to proceed. Theoretically he could just tell the mummy what to do. Theoretically.

Bert stepped out into the open. "Excuse me. Mummy person? Bert here to fight you."

Brotep shrieked. The mummy scrambled backwards, kicking up sand as he sought to escape. He kept backpedaling until he ran into the wall, and only then did he look around.

"Mummy person!" Bert called, waving his arms. "Over here."

The mummy finally rose slowly to his feet, and retrieved one of the gold chains he'd dropped in the sand. He peered suspiciously in Bert's direction, from under his wrappings. "Are you—a critter? Why do you feel so powerful?" The mummy moved cautiously closer, but still looked like he might run. "Oh, my—you're the dark lord?"

The mummy sank to his knees, his wrappings rustling as he settled into the sand. Then the mummy prostrated himself. "Dark Lord, please tell me you've returned to kill the ass-clowns upstairs. Having white wizards in the throne room is an insult to every dark lord that ever terrorized this region."

"Uh, sure," Bert agreed. He did want to kill White after all. "Bert need help though. Mummy person need to tell cats not to hurt friends."

"You've brought more minions?" Brotep rose to his knees. "Of course you would. I'll remove my children and allow your minions to pass. What else do you require, Lord?"

"Umm." Bert considered that. He needed Crotchshot. Should he ask for the rest of the adventurers that had been turned to stone? No, probably not. They'd be an unknown quantity, and they might not work together. Too complicated. "Bert need you to wake up ranger guy. Can show you, if needed."

"My newest piece?" Brotep blinked those cracked, rheumy eyes. "Well, I don't like giving up parts of my collection, but if you think it necessary..."

"Bert does." Bert nodded emphatically. "Wake up ranger. Bert go get friends. Come back. Kill White."

"Thank you, Lord." The mummy prostrated himself again. It made Bert a little uncomfortable.

He hurried from the room, back toward his friends. That mummy thought he was evil. Bert was fairly certain of it. Being a dark lord was complicated. He didn't like pretending to be something he wasn't, but that seemed like the smartest way to win.

Bert would just tell the mummy the truth after they'd dealt with the necromancer. After all, he was in charge. So the mummy would have to listen to him.

Bert had minions. He was kind of a big deal now.

36

AMBUSH

Kit adjusted her pack so that the disintegrate scroll was close at hand. Stepping back into that sand-filled room took a great deal of willpower, especially since she was in elf form, which made her slower, and a great deal more visible.

There was no sign of Jenna, though Kit was fairly certain the rogue was lurking in the shadows behind a nearby obelisk. She hoped so, anyway.

"Is okay," Bert whispered loudly into her ear from his perch on her shoulder. "Mummy will do what Bert say."

When the mummy stepped into view she very nearly bolted.

It was the first time she'd gotten a good look at the thing. His wrappings were dark with age, though the cloth seemed preserved past a certain point. A dozen or more gold chains hung around his neck, many with amulets at the end. The oddest feature was the sunglasses, and the strange hat with a duck-like bill, angled forty-five degrees off center.

"You must be the dark lord's new minions." The mummy moonwalked over, and started beatboxing while he performed a strange dance. He stopped, and gave a bow. "I'm Brotep. If you think we're gonna be bros you can call me Ramen, but no one does that."

Jenna advanced cautiously, but only a little. She kept a good dozen paces between her and the mummy, and looked ready to flee.

"I'm Kit," she managed, mouth dry. "I'm, uh, the dark lord's sorceress. This is Jenna, the dark lord's rogue. We need to collect his ranger, and we're told you were going to free him."

"Oh, yeah, I was, wasn't I? No worries, won't take but a sec." Brotep walked through the room with purpose, threading a path between dozens of statues. He stopped at one Kit recognized, Crotchshot's blissful expression forever locked into place. "Okay, stand back. And bear in mind he's gonna be a little disoriented from the granite sickness."

Brotep touched two fingers to the statue's forehead, and began beatboxing again. The beat went on for some time, and Kit found herself nodding along. He really was quite skilled. The mummy started bobbing as he performed, then abruptly stopped both the dancing and the beat.

"He's coming to." The mummy took a step back and folded his arms.

Patches of Crotchshot's statue began to glow, and a warbling hum filled the room. The patches grew, slowly spreading across the surface of the statue. Each patch glowed a brilliant gold, until the light had covered the entire statue. It exploded outwards in a wave, and when the light cleared Crotchshot had been restored.

Well, mostly restored. His hair had turned stark white, and now jutted out at odd angles, as if he'd been electrocuted. His eyes were unfocused, and his expression shifted from bliss to terror. "Wait, what just happened? I'm blind!

Why can't I see anything? Brakestuff, bud, I need a restoration, man."

"It's okay," Kit called. She hurried to the ranger's side, and wrapped an arm around him. "It's Kit. You're safe. I'll catch you up on everything that's happened, but you're not going to like it."

Crotchshot tensed. "Why not?"

"It's been a few weeks," Kit explained. "White used you as bait, and you were petrified. White didn't care. Neither did Brakestuff. They abandoned you."

"They...left me?" Crotchshot shook his head. "White would, sure, but Brakestuff left me? That stings."

"Then you're definitely not going to like this next part," Kit continued. "White joined the OLP, and they've been persecuting all non-good creatures. The elves were wiped out, and so were the orcs. Even the goblins were hard hit."

"But I'm neutral," he protested. Crotchshot rose shakily to his feet. "Not evil. If we're not evil why do they want us dead?"

"White's justification was that we can fall from grace, and he wants to preemptively prevent that from happening." Kit shook her head in disgust. She could feel Bert's tension, and his little hand tightened on her collar until the knuckles went white. "Even you're not safe. He might exile you, like he did me. Or he might kill you outright. Brake is going along with it all, which makes sense since White restored the temple of Knowsbest."

"Well, shit." Crotchshot blinked a few times. "At least I'm starting to see a little light now. Y'all are blobs, but at least you're different shapes. So what now? We escaping, or killing them all and then escaping?"

"We kill all," Bert growled. "Then Bert take over."

Crotchshot didn't seem to hear the goblin, so Kit

supplied her own answer. "We're going to take them down. Starting with Brakestuff. It's still pretty early in the morning, and he's almost certainly still in bed."

"You want to ambush him in bed?" Crotchshot reached over his shoulder and slowly drew an arrow, which he nocked on the bowstring. He gave a slow smile. "That's probably the smartest route. We can kill him before he gets into his armor. His AC is out of reach, otherwise. What other resources we got? I see another dark shape. Looks like a lady. Is she hot? I can't make out shit."

"I'm Jenna," the were-cougar purred. She sauntered over to Crotchshot and his whole body language shifted in her direction. "I've heard stories. They say you're utterly ruthless, and that you never miss."

"Yeah. I'm kind of a badass." Crotchshot tried to look cool, but the mussed hair ruined the image. "I'm pretty ruthless. And it's true that I never miss. The bow is cursed."

"Mummy person," Bert called. He pointed at Crotchshot. "How long 'til granite sickness gone?"

"Shouldn't be more than a few minutes."

Bert turned to Kit. "How far to dwarf's room?"

"It's a bit of a hike," Kit said. "We should get moving." She turned to Jenna. "Help Crotchshot until he's able to move under his own power."

"Gladly," she purred, and wrapped an arm around the ranger. "Right this way. You put your hands anywhere you need to. No wrong answers."

Kit started up the corridor. "Let's get moving. The longer we're here the greater the chance Brakestuff will wake up. It's late morning. He likes to sleep in, but eventually he'll want breakfast. Crotchshot, you're sure you're up to this?"

"You bet your ass I am." The ranger's eyes blazed. "Bastard turned on me. I'll shoot that righteous little prick right in the prick."

Kit felt better knowing he was committed. She threaded unerringly through the tomb, guiding the others on the fastest route to Brake's quarters. He'd taken rooms not far from White's, though odds were extremely high that White was already in the throne room bragging to his fellow OLP members. They'd be bragging back. It was like a bunch of seagulls all screaming at the same time.

In theory, that meant Brakestuff was as vulnerable as he'd ever be.

She slowed as they reached the corner to the corridor his rooms occupied. She heard nothing, so she crept up the cold stone and stopped outside of the oaken door barring his quarters. It was thick enough that it would muffle what little sound she created, and Jenna created even less.

"Gather around," Kit whispered, just outside the door. She waited for Jenna and Crotchshot to approach, then dropped her voice to a bare breath. "I'm going to cast haste. After I do that, I'll open the door. Crotch, take your best shot. When Brake moves to engage you, Jenna will sneak attack him. Hit him as hard as you can."

"What Bert do?" he whispered, louder than the rest of them. Bert's eyes widened and he clapped his hands over his mouth.

"Nothing, initially." Kit settled one hand on the door, and set her staff against the wall so she'd have the other to cast haste. "If we get into trouble, then I want you to point at Brake and say die."

Bert blinked at her. "Will work? Bert point and dwarf die?"

Kit nodded gravely. "It will work, but I don't know how many times you can cast it. I want you to save it for White."

Bert nodded. "Make sense. Bert will be backup."

"Okay, here goes." Kit whispered her haste spell, and the magic rippled out over the party. "Now!" She yanked the door open, and Crotchshot was the first one through.

Jenna flowed into the room next, her form disappearing into the shadows. Kit caught a strong whiff of cat, and realized that Jenna must have shifted.

A raucous snoring came from a four-poster bed in the center of the room. It was shrouded in shadow, minus what little torchlight slipped in through the doorway. Thankfully, elves could see in the dark, and she knew Crotchshot would have no trouble making the shot.

As if on cue a bowstring twanged. Once, twice, and third time in quick succession. A hissing split the air, and then a roar of immense pain began at the same moment the snoring stopped. "Ahh, my bloody crotch!" The naked dwarf rolled from bed, and grabbed a battle axe from the nightstand. "You just did forty-one points of damage. I'll teach you to—"

Three more twangs, and a moment later the dwarf bellowed again. He rolled behind the bed and took cover. "Thirty-six bloody points of damage? I hate having a low AC." The dwarf glared over the bed, his unruly hair poking out above him. "Only one man would shoot me there. Crotchshot, how'd you get out of the petrification? Listen, I get that you're a little angry—"

"A little angry?" Crotchshot's comically high-pitched voice held an edge Kit had never heard. He was furious. "You left me to rot, Brake. You and White both."

"Yeah, well…" Brake yanked an arrow from his crotch with a grunt. "Abandoning you was a real pity, but my god has spoken. I mean, it's what my character would do." The dwarf's eyes hardened. "I'm going to take you down. For good this time, Crotch. And then I'm going to break that bow in half. And your next character had better be good. Too much party strife otherwise. The games aren't fun."

"Take me down? Oh, I don't think so." Crotch gave a cruel smile.

"And why's that? You can shoot me—"

Twang, twang, twang. Three more arrows slammed into the dwarf, and Brake stumbled backward. "Gonna take more than..."

Sharp feline claws flashed in the darkness from behind the dwarf, and slashed deep into his throat. The dwarf didn't stand a chance as the cougar mauled him, as she'd no doubt done to many other victims.

Jenna raked his throat one last time, then the tawny cat bounded off into the darkness, leaving the dwarf to die. Brakestuff reached up weakly with both hands to staunch the flow of blood from his throat, "You bastard. When we get back to the real world I'm going to do some live action role-play. My foot is the cursed bow, and your crotch is, well, your crotch."

"Hey, we've got rules, man." Crotchshot loosed another trio of arrows, which streaked unerringly toward their target. Crotchshot winced as they slammed home. "What happens in game, stays in game." Then he fired again.

Kit turned from the carnage with a wince. She almost pitied the dwarf, but she hardened her heart. This had to be done, and besides he'd be back with an equally sanctimonious character in the next adventure.

Now, it was time to kill White.

37

CLIMACTIC BATTLE

K it's hands were shaking as their ragged little
party made its way up the corridor toward the
throne room. She scarcely believed that taking
down Brakestuff could have been that easy. Kit had spent so
much time living in fear of the paladin, because his support
of White was what had really cemented the necromancer's
power.

She'd seen Brake stand toe-to-toe with ancient wyrms
and armies of undead. In the end all it had taken to kill him
was an ambush, which now that she thought about it was
probably why their original adventuring party won so much
of the time. Even dragons didn't survive waking up to a
cluster of arrows to the crotch and an axe to the face, delivered by fully buffed adventurers.

"What plan?" Bert whispered, loud enough to carry.

Kit froze and everyone else pulled up short next to her.
She realized that, for good or ill, she was the leader of this
little group. She was filling the role that White had in her
last group, though where he'd loved the power and control,
she found it terrifying.

"When the door opens," she whispered, a bare breath, "Bert will sneak up to the throne, where White will undoubtedly be sitting. We know he's likely to have all three OLP wizards with him, and Sir Patrick, so we're going to have to engage them until Bert can take care of White."

She licked her lips. Did she need to give individual combat orders? She wasn't qualified to do that. "Crotchshot, Jenna, focus your attacks. Pick off targets one by one. I'll haste us before we go in, and then I'll counter every spell I can to keep us up as long as possible. Questions?"

Everyone shook their heads. Crotchshot looked far more serious than she ever remembered seeing him, the gravity of killing a former friend carving deep lines of concern on his face. It was the closest to real roleplaying that he'd ever demonstrated, on this character or any other.

Jenna quietly observed them all, but showed no hint of emotion.

And Bert was Bert, humming quietly to himself on her shoulder, a habit she realized he displayed when thinking about something he considered important.

"All right. Let's do this." Kit raised her hand and quietly cast a haste spell. Not quietly enough.

"Master White," boomed Sir Patrick's voice from behind the thick oaken door. "I hear someone preparing a haste spell. Begin your buff spells. I will keep them at bay while you and the other wizards prepare their deaths."

So much for surprise.

"*Explodi-omus!*" Kit yelled, and the door to the throne room burst inward in a spray of wooden shards.

Crotchshot was already in motion, three arrows appearing on his bowstring one after another as he glided into the room. All three arrows made for the closest wizard, who Kit guessed might be Gonedeaf. The wizard's eyes widened, and his mouth started to open, but by then the first arrow had hit.

Gonedeaf stumbled backward, but Jenna gave him no quarter. She leapt into the air, shifting as she flew, and came down on the wizard in a storm of fangs and teeth. The wizard was woefully unprepared, and went down screaming, blood drenching the wall behind him as the cougar mauled him.

A moment later blue magic rippled through the room, and the surviving wizards were augmented by a haste spell, cast by Bumbledork. Merlin took a more offensive tact, and threw a fireball from the tip of his long, black rod.

Kit instinctively raised a hand to counter, but realized that if she did she'd be unprepared for whatever White was going to do. She decided she feared White's theoretical spell a great deal more than the fireball.

The ball sailed almost lazily into their midst, and then mushroomed outward in an explosion of force and heat. The magical flame billowed out around Kit, searing her skin and hair, and blinding her temporarily.

When the flames passed she blinked past the pain, ignoring the tears streaming down her scorched skin. She focused on White, just in time to see him begin casting.

White raised an aged scroll and intoned the letters from the page, "*Vos meliora habebat contra leporem!*"

Kit's hand came up, and she cast a dispel magic at the pool of dark energy gathering above the scroll. Her counter-spell slammed into it, and the scroll went up in sudden flames, the spell dissipating harmlessly around White in a puff of brimstone.

Rage boiled onto the necromancer's face, but he didn't rise from his throne. "End them! End them now!"

Bumbledork's hand swept up, and a globe of minor invulnerability sprang up around White's throne. The wizard frantically stumbled into the iridescent sphere, and moved to stand behind the throne.

Crotchshot loosed another trio of arrows, but they pinged off the translucent grey bubble. Jenna prowled around the outside of it, unable to find a way inside.

Kit gave a cruel smile, and was immensely grateful for the trope she'd been given. The lesser sphere of invulnerability blocked all physical damage, and some spells. But not higher level ones. More importantly, the bubble was atmospherically contained, to protect the caster from toxins.

Unless someone cast those toxins directly inside the sphere. Kit yanked the cloudkill scroll from her bag, and cracked the seal. She raised it, and quickly chanted the words. At first there was no effect, visibly at least.

Kit felt the pulse of magic as the spell completed, but it didn't manifest until a thick, mustard-colored mist billowed out from the center of the sphere. Bumbledork began to choke and gag, and collapsed into the fog, either dead or incapacitated. Merlin raised a hand, sketched a spell, and vanished.

For a single instant she believed they were winning, and then Sir Patrick rammed his great sword through Crotchshot's midsection, pinning the ranger to the wall. Jenna clawed at the knight's face, but he backhanded the cougar away, and returned to dismembering Crotchshot.

Kit scanned her spell list, but she couldn't think of anything that would stop a death knight.

The air popped and spun behind her, quickly resolving into Merlin, his smug smile directed firmly at Kit. Merlin held a small oaken wand clutched tightly in one fist, and the end of that wand had begun to glow with the telltale scarlet of a disintegrate.

Kit was about to die. She started to raise her hand to begin a counterspell, but it was far, far too late. She closed her eyes and accepted the inevitable. It had been a good run. She'd almost made it to tenth level.

38

EVIL NECROMANCER PERSON

ert did exactly as Kit instructed, not just because she'd asked, but because it was the smartest way to stay alive. He scurried around the edge of the room, and had he not walked as fast as his legs would allow he'd have been caught in the area of effect when the fireball detonated in the doorway.

As it was he could feel the heat wash over him, and was acutely aware of having only a single hit point. He'd gotten lucky, and he didn't want to count on that again.

Bert waded through the chaos, and ducked under a sword swipe as Sir Patrick charged at Crotchshot. He kept his head down and circled the outer edge of the room, slowly approaching the big, black throne near the center of the back wall.

White sat atop it, a spider in its web, glaring arrogantly at the people who'd defiled his throne room. Bert liked that word, defiled. He redoubled his pace, and finally reached the throne itself. White still hadn't noticed him.

Bert began climbing the arm of the throne, and slowly pulled himself up. He slipped, but his shirt caught on a demon's horn, and prevented him from falling very far. Bert got himself under control, and continued to climb.

After what felt like a long time he finally reached the right arm of the chair, and pulled himself atop it. This close to White the odor of his robes was apparent, and Bert noted that what had once begun as white cloth was now almost entirely black, coated by a layer of grime and blood.

A sudden popping came from the air behind Bert, and he instinctively dove for cover. He almost toppled off the side of the arm, but managed to catch himself against the demon's horns etched into the metal.

The popping had been caused by one of the wizards suddenly reappearing. He stood behind Kit, and raised a wand. The end began to glow with a malevolent ruby light, and grew brighter as the wizard intoned the words to a terrible spell.

Bert glanced up at Master White, who sat grinning in the throne. He seemed certain of victory, and Bert's newfound intellect agreed. They were losing, and it put him in an impossible position. Bert could tell exactly one person to die, and they would. He understood the ramifications of Power Word: Kill, part of the dark lord trope no doubt.

He could use that ability on Master White right now, but if he did so Kit would die. An evil dark lord wouldn't care. White wouldn't care. But Bert cared. Bert only had a few friends, and he wasn't going to lose any of them.

Bert pointed up at Merlin, his arm impossibly slow as it raced the glow of the wand. What if the wizard couldn't hear him? Did that matter? He was still a critter. What if the ability failed? He was about to find out.

"Excuse me, evil wizard person," Bert bellowed at the top of his tiny lungs. There was no response. The glow grew, and he somehow sensed that the spell was about to discharge. "*Die!*"

A ray of crackling energy shot from Bert's finger, blacker than death and twice as cold. It shot into the wizard's back, and rippled outward across his entire body. The wizard's wand began to tremble, them tumbled from limp fingers.

The wizard sagged to his knees, his skin growing mottled and even more aged, until it was as thin as an old sandwich wrapper. The wizard toppled forward, and went limp. His eyes stared sightlessly at the wall, and a single ragged sigh escaped his lungs, then he was still.

Bert turned to face Master White, both elated that Kit was still alive, and ashamed that he'd used their one weapon so foolishly. Now White was likely to kill them all. It infuriated Bert. Absolutely infuriated him. Helping your friends shouldn't mean that you lost.

His tiny hands balled into fists, and he glared up at White from his perch on the edge of the throne.

"Evil necromancer person!" Bert shouted, as loudly and fiercely as any goblin had ever shouted. "Excuse me!"

White straightened on his throne, and his jaw fell open as he stared down at Merlin's still cooling corpse. "How did you? No matter. I'll finish this myself." The necromancer raised a hand and began to cast some sort of spell.

Bert acted quickly. He unslung his pack from his shoulder, and shoved a hand inside. It settled around something cold and metal, and he withdrew a copper piece that must have been mixed in with the gold.

He leaned back and put his entire body into the motion, then rocked forward and hurled the copper piece at White's face. It sailed into his temple, and bonked off, just lightly enough to get the necromancer's attention.

"Evil necromancer see Bert now?" Bert demanded. He

planted his hands on his hips in his best imitation of his mother.

White blinked down at him, and his jaw worked as if grinding up the words into small enough pieces to escape. He seemed utterly bewildered, for several long seconds.

Bert seized the initiative, and stabbed a finger up at White. "You evil. You kill my people. Kill elves, and orcs, and trolls. You kill Stella. Bert not care what alignment say. You evil! Even robes are black."

White began to laugh. It started slowly, a quick chuckle of disbelief, but it grew into a wheezing laughter that caused tears to stream down White's angular face. He wiped a tear, then mastered himself enough to speak. "I'm being condemned by a critter. How unexpected. Every time I think I have this game figured out I learn something new. Critters are much more important than expected, as evidenced by you stealing my trope. I can think of so many ways to exploit them. So many loopholes."

White stared down at Bert's chest in naked avarice.

Bert glanced down at the darkly glowing trope, and then back up at White. The answer was there. He was certain of it. There was a way to stop White, and it didn't have to be the word of power. He didn't even need to use a minion, though Bert briefly considered taking control of the death knight, who'd finished goring Crotchshot.

The ranger's broken body slumped against the wall, his eyes staring sightlessly ahead. The battle's first real casualty on their side. No, Sir Patrick might be strong, but White was uniquely suited to dealing with minions like him. Bert needed another answer.

"You evil," Bert repeated, but with more certainty now. He cocked his head to the side, and studied White. The necromancer was surrounded by a sort of...aura. It lay just beyond him, a separate layer of reality that Bert could peel back if he wanted.

Bert scanned that aura, shocked to discover not only words, but a logical system of attributes, skills, and abilities. It showed every component that made up White, right down to the seventh level White Necromancer representing his class.

One of those bits of data leapt out from the others. Alignment: Lawful Good. Bert looked at White, the epitome of evil, and then at that bit of data. It wasn't right. A mistake had been made somehow.

In that moment Bert understood the true power of the dark lord trope, and why it was so vital, and so powerful. The person with the trope could alter the game as needed, in order to best present challenges to adventurers.

That meant Bert could change things, things he didn't think were right. Like White's alignment. Bert willed it to become correct, or what he considered correct. The letters shimmered out of existence, and in their place the words neutral evil appeared.

Bert smiled cruelly, then turned back to the room. Jenna was clawing at Sir Patrick's ghostly face, and Kit was desperately defending herself in a magical duel with Bumbledork, her old headmaster as Bert understood it. Not that he knew what a headmaster was, precisely. Something like G. Mayor, but for a big school? He made a mental note to find out later.

"Wizard person!" Bert yelled, and this time he used the magic of the trope. It infused his words, making the walls tremble from the deafening sound. Bert blinked as all eyes settled on him. Wow, he was really loud now. Bert lowered his voice to a whisper, so as not to hurt his own ears. "Wizard person, see necromancer?" Bert pointed at

White. "Necromancer evil. Wizard supposed to kill, right?"

Bumbledork's eyes widened, and he stepped dramatically backward as he raised his wand in a defensive stance. "The true dark lord! I see it now. I have been taken in by your sorcery, but no longer." His wand began to glow with a very similar spell to what he'd had been trying to cast on Kit, and he intoned strange words that Bert almost understood. "*Ardvarka Kedavra!*"

White raised his hand to cast, but Kit was faster.

"Oh, no, you don't!" Kit's hand came up, and White's spell broke apart as she countered it.

That left him vulnerable to the killing curse that shot from Bumbledork's wand into his chest. Ruby energy pulsed through White's body, and Bert watched in awe as his hit points were reduced to zero on the character sheet.

White's body slumped against the throne, and some of the tension ebbed out of Bert. He sat on the edge of the throne's arm, and blinked at White's corpse. The corpse blinked back.

White sat up in the throne, and delivered a truly ghastly, undead smile. "You didn't think it would be that easy, did you? I've long since prepared for this character's death. You've only made me stronger. Now, I'm a lich! My power is beyond your—"

"Lich is monster, right?" Bert interrupted. He folded his arms and stared cagily up at the newly minted lich.

"If you want to get technical," White allowed with a shrug. "My subtype is now undead, which is a monster—"

"Monsters do what Bert say," Bert pointed at him smugly. "You monster. Lich cast spells, right?"

"Yes." White's voice had become very small, almost as small as Bert.

"You know disintegrate?" Bert asked. He'd heard Kit mention that she was worried White might cast that spell.

"Yes." White's voice was so faint Bert could barely make it out, but he caught White's faint nod.

"Good." Bert walked a few steps closer, as close as he could get without falling off the throne's arm. He stared up at White, and he said all the things he'd wanted to say. "You make people feel small. Bert watch you for months. You mean to Crotchshot, and you make Brakestuff feel stupid. But worse than that? You mean to Kit. Kit was better wizard than you ever be. Apologize."

White's expression melted into horror. His mouth seemed to move of its own accord, and the words hardly matched the expression. "I'm sorry, Kit."

"Good. Now disintegrate self." Bert folded his arms again, and stared reprovingly at the necromancer. Reprovingly was a good word.

"Please," White begged, his voice all anguish, just as Bert's people had felt.

"Necromancer heard Bert. Kill self." Bert frowned sternly up at the necromancer, and felt not an ounce of pity.

White chanted in that strange language, and a bolt of dark scarlet energy shot from his finger into his own chest. It rippled outwards, darkening his entire body until it seemed to drink in light. Then it exploded into sudden brilliance as a sea of particles dissolved around the area where White had been. When it faded, there was nothing left but the tattered remains of his greasy robe.

Bert hopped down onto the throne, and kicked the robe onto the floor. He reached into his pack, and extracted his broom, then quickly swept bits of necromancer off his new seat. Finally, Bert sat down and faced his friends.

"Bert did it!" He pumped his fists high up in the air. "Now Bert Dark Lord."

Kit began to laugh, but it was a fun, relieved laugh. The kind of laugh shared by friends.

Bert began to laugh as well.

EPILOGUE

Kit's body rippled, and her perspective changed as she resumed her elven form. Relief flooded her as she stared at White's curiously lifeless body, which Sir Patrick had unceremoniously dumped on the stone in front of Bert's new throne.

The goblin sat in the center of the throne, but he was too small to rest his hands on the arms. His little feet dangled off the side, and he stared owlishly around the room, as if unable to believe what was happening. She empathized.

Crotchshot's body lay where he'd fallen, a mass of blood and gore. She experienced a moment of uncharacteristic sadness, the kind she didn't usually feel for his characters. He'd actually role-played on this one, and she hoped that his next character would be even better.

Jenna's were-cougar form rippled in a familiar way, and the blonde was suddenly standing in the cat's place, a pair of wicked daggers clutched in her hands. She stared down at Crotchshot's body, and gave a sad shake of her head. "Pity. I would have mauled him once we got back to my inn room. Ah well, guess it's back to the bartender. How are we divvying up loot? This guy's probably got a ton of stuff. Rings, amulets, headband, cloak. He's got something in every slot."

"Yes, Kit," Bumbledork chimed in, "who's getting what? You're running party loot now, right? As everyone else is dead, that's us."

Kit was taken aback. They wanted her opinion. She knew what White would do. He'd take what he wanted, and leave them scraps, which he'd forced them to pay for with shares of party treasure. White was an asshole.

"I'm going to take this." Kit bent and picked up one of White's hands. It was still warm. She removed the ring of wizardry from his index finger, then slid it around her finger. "Bert, you're next. Then Jenna, and Bumbledork."

"I go after a critter?" Jenna delivered a scandalized look.

"Bert dark lord," the goblin pointed out. He patted the trope in his chest. "Plus Kit sort by seniority. Bert been here longer. You new girl."

Jenna's shoulders slumped. "That's true. I am the new girl. Maybe I should change my name to Jess."

Kit didn't pay much attention as they descended on White's body like locusts. They went round robin, and when her next turn came she took White's haversack. She'd always been jealous of his magical bag, and now she had one.

The looting frenzy went on for some time, and when it was finally over everyone seemed more or less content, despite standing in the midst of carnage. Blood spattered the walls, and multiple dead wizards dotted the room.

"What Kit do now?" Bert asked. He peered up at her from the enormous throne. "Bert need help running kingdom. Bert also want to learn magic."

A powerful weariness washed over Kit, but it brought

with it a wave of contentment. "For now? We've beaten two dark lords, and come away with a pile of treasure. I guess I'm going to take a break before the next adventure. I need to get back to my real life for a while. How about you?"

Bert folded his hands in his lap, and eyed her seriously. "Bert want to make city better. Help everyone. Fix stuff. But Bert scared. More adventurers will come."

Kit nodded soberly. "And they won't be the only ones. Other dark lords will hear about you soon enough, and they may want to take what you have. But even if they don't, White will just make another character, and so will Brakestuff. They're not going to be happy. White will hold a grudge."

Bert sighed. "Being dark lord complicated."

"I imagine it will be, but you know what? I think you'll do a better job of it than any of the others." Kit looked around the battle-scarred throne room one last time, then gave Bert an affectionate pat on the shoulder. Somewhere the real world was waiting for her, with its myriad responsibilities and problems. She was reluctant to return, but she'd finished her adventure here.

She meant what she'd said though. She'd be back soon enough, and she couldn't wait to see what Bert changed in the game while she was gone. She had a feeling that the world wasn't ready for the Dark Lord Bert.

Want more info on book releases, character artwork and other goodies? Check out my website at chrisfoxwrites.com

If you'd like to visit me on Facebook you can find me at https://www.facebook.com/chrisfoxwrites

38482007R00121

Printed in Poland
by Amazon Fulfillment
Poland Sp. z o.o., Wrocław